Pierre Souvestre, Marcel Allain

A Royal Prisoner: Fantômas Saga

OK Publishing 2021

Pierre Souvestre, Marcel Allain
A Royal Prisoner: Fantômas Saga

Published by
MUSAICUM
Books

- Advanced Digital Solutions & High-Quality book Formatting -

musaicumbooks@okpublishing.info

2021 OK Publishing

ISBN 978-80-272-7888-6

Contents

CHAPTER I
A ROYAL JAG

"After all, why not celebrate? It's the last day of the year and it won't come again for twelve months."

It was close upon midnight.

Jerome Fandor, reporter on the popular newspaper, *La Capitale*, was strolling along the boulevard; he had just come from a banquet, one of those official and deadly affairs at which the guests are obliged to listen to interminable speeches. He had drowsed through the evening and at the first opportunity had managed to slip away quickly.

The theatres were just out and the boulevard was crowded with people intent on making a night of it. Numberless automobiles containing the fashionable and rich of Paris blocked the streets. The restaurants were brilliantly illuminated, and as carriages discharged their occupants before the doors, one glimpsed the neat feet and ankles of daintily clad women as they crossed the sidewalk and disappeared inside, following their silk-hatted escorts, conscious of their own importance.

Many years of active service in Paris as chief reporter of *La Capitale* had brought Jerome Fandor in touch with a good third of those who constitute Parisian society, and rarely did he fail to exchange a nod, a smile, or half a dozen words of friendly greeting whenever he set foot out of doors.

But in spite of his popularity he led a lonely life — many acquaintances, but few close friends. The great exception was Juve, the celebrated detective.

In fact, Fandor's complex and adventurous life was very much bound up with that of the police officer, for they had worked together in solving the mystery of many tragic crimes.

On this particular evening, the reporter became gradually imbued with the general spirit of gaiety and abandon which surrounded him.

"Hang it," he muttered, "I might go and hunt up Juve and drag him off to supper, but I'm afraid I should get a cool reception if I did. He is probably sleeping the sleep of the just and would strongly object to being disturbed. Anyway, sooner or later, I'll probably run into some one I know."

On reaching Drouet Square, he espied an inviting-looking restaurant, brilliantly lit. He was about to make his way to a table when the head waiter stopped him.

"Your name, please!"

"What's that?" replied Fandor.

The waiter answered with ironical politeness:

"I take it for granted you have engaged a table. We haven't a single vacant place left."

Fandor had the same luck at several other restaurants and then began to suffer the pangs of hunger, having, on principle, scarcely touched the heavy dishes served at the banquet.

After wandering aimlessly about, he walked toward the Madeleine and turned off into the Rue Royale in the direction of the Faubourg Saint-Honoré.

As he was passing a discreet looking restaurant with many thick velvet curtains and an imposing array of private automobiles before it, he heard his name called.

He stopped short and turned to see a vision of feminine loveliness standing before him.

"Isabelle de Guerray!" he cried.

"And how are you, my dear boy? Come along in with me."

Fandor had known Isabelle de Guerray when she was a young school teacher just graduated from Sévres. Her career, beginning with a somewhat strange and unorthodox affair with a young man of good family who had killed himself for her, had progressed by rapid strides and her name was frequently cited in the minor newspapers as giving elegant "society" suppers, the guests being usually designated by their initials!

Fandor remarked that the fair Isabelle seemed to be putting on weight, especially round the shoulders and hips, but she still retained a great deal of dash and an ardent look in her eyes, very valuable assets in her profession.

"I have my table here, at Raxim's, you must come and join us," and she added with a sly smile, "Oh — quite platonically — I know you're unapproachable."

A deafening racket was going on in the narrow, oblong room. The habitués of the place all knew each other and the conversation was general. No restraint was observed, so that it was quite permissible to wander about, hat on head and cigar between lips, or take a lady upon one's knees.

Fandor followed Isabelle to a table overloaded with flowers and bottles of champagne. Here and there he recognized old friends from the Latin Quarter or Montmartre, among them Conchita Conchas, a Spanish dancer in vogue the previous winter. A tiny woman, who might have been a girl of fifteen from her figure, but whose face was marked with the lines of dissipation, ran into him and Fandor promptly put his arm round her waist.

"Hello, if it isn't little Souppe!"

"Paws down or I'll scratch," was the sharp reply.

The next moment he was shaking hands with Daisy Kissmi, an English girl who had become quite a feature of Raxim's.

Further on he noticed a pale, bald, and already pot-bellied young man, who was staring with lack-lustre eyes at his whiskey and soda. This premature ruin was listening distraitly to a waiter who murmured mysteriously into his ear.

At the end of the room, surrounded by pretty women, sat the old Duke de Pietra, descendant of a fine old Italian family, and near him Arnold, an actor from the music halls.

The patrons had no choice in regard to the supper, which was settled by the head waiter. Each received a bottle of champagne, Ostend oysters, and, later, large slices of *pâté de foie gras*, and as the bottles were emptied, intoxication became general, while even the waiters seemed to catch the spirit of abandon. When the Hungarian band had played their most seductive waltzes, the leader came forward to the middle of the room and announced a new piece of his own composition, called "The Singing Fountains." This met with instant applause and laughter.

As the night wore on the noise became positively deafening. A young Jew named Weil invented a new game. He seized two plates and began scraping them together. Many of the diners followed his example.

"Look here," exclaimed Conchita Conchas, leaning familiarly upon Fandor's shoulder, "why don't you give us tickets for to-morrow to hear these famous Fountains?"

Fandor started to explain that the young woman would be in bed and sound asleep when that event took place, but the Spanish girl, without waiting for the answer, had strolled away.

The journalist rose with the intention of making his escape, when a voice directly behind him made him pause.

"Excuse me, but you seem to know all about these 'Singing Fountains.' Will you kindly explain to me what they are? I am a stranger in the city."

Fandor turned and saw a man of about thirty, fair-haired, with a heavy moustache, seated alone at a small table. The stranger was well built and of distinguished appearance. The journalist suppressed a start of amazement.

"Why, it's not surprising that you have not heard of them, they are quite unimportant. On the Place de la Concorde there are two bronze monuments representing Naiads emerging from the fountains. You probably have seen them yourself?"

The stranger nodded, and poured out another glass of champagne.

"Well," continued Fandor, "recently passers-by have fancied they heard sounds coming from these figures. In fact, they declare that the Naiads have been singing. A delightfully poetic and thoroughly Parisian idea, isn't it?"

"Very Parisian indeed."

"The papers have taken it up, and one you probably know by name, *La Capitale*, has decided to investigate this strange phenomenon."

"What was Conchita asking you just now?"

"Oh, nothing, merely to give her a card for the ceremony."

The conversation continued and turned to other subjects. The stranger ordered more wine and insisted on Fandor joining him. He seemed to be particularly interested in the subject of women and the night life of Paris.

"If only I could persuade him to come with me," thought Fandor. "I'd show him a stunt or two, and what a scoop it would make ... if it could be printed! He certainly is drunk, very drunk, and that may help me."

On the Place de la Concorde, deserted at this late hour, two men, arm in arm, were taking their devious way. They were Fandor and the stranger he had met at Raxim's.

The journalist, with the aid of an extra bottle, had persuaded his new friend to finish the night among the cafés of Montmartre. The sudden change from the overheated restaurant to the cold outside increased the effects of the alcohol and Fandor realized that he himself was far from sober. As his companion seemed to be obsessed with the idea of seeing the Fountains, the journalist piloted him to the Place de la Concorde.

"There you are," he exclaimed, "but you see they're closed. No more singing to-night. Now come and have a drink."

"Good idea, some more champagne."

Fandor hailed a taxi, and ordered the chauffeur to drive to the Place Pigalle. As he was shutting the door, he observed an old beggar, who evidently was afraid to ask for alms. Fandor threw him a coin as the taxi started.

It was three in the morning, and the Place Pigalle was crowded with carriages, porters and a constant ebb and flow of all sorts of people.

The journalist and his companion emerged some time later from one of the best known restaurants, both drunk, especially the stranger, who could scarcely keep his feet.

"Look here, we must go ... go...."

"Go to bed," interrupted Fandor.

"No. I know where we can go...."

"But we've been everywhere."

"We'll go to my rooms ... to her rooms ... to Susy d'Orsel ... she's my girl ... d'ye know, she's been expecting me for supper since midnight."

"More supper?"

"Of course ... there's plenty of room left."

With some difficulty the stranger managed to give the address, 247 Rue de Monceau.

"All right," said Fandor to himself, "we'll have some fun; after all, what do I risk?"

While the taxi shook them violently from side to side, Fandor grew comparatively sober. He examined his companion more closely and was surprised to see how well he carried himself in spite of his condition.

"Well," he summed up, "he certainly has a jag, but it's a royal jag!"

CHAPTER II
MOTHER CITRON'S TENANTS

"Now you've forgotten the fish knives and forks! Do you expect my lover to eat with his fingers like that old Chinaman I had for three months last year!"

Susy d'Orsel spoke with a distinct accent of the Faubourg, which contrasted strangely with her delicate and distinguished appearance.

Justine, her maid, stood staring in reply.

"But, Madame, we have lobsters...."

"What's that got to do with it, they're fish, ain't they?"

The young woman left the table and went into the adjoining room, a small drawing-room, elegantly furnished in Louis XV style.

"Justine," she called.

"Madame."

"Here's another mistake. You mustn't get red orchids. Throw these out....I want either mauve or yellow ones....You know those are the official colors of His Majesty."

"Queer taste his ... His Majesty has for yellow."

"What's that to do with you. Get a move on, lay the table."

"I left the *pâté de foie gras* in the pantry with ice round it."

"All right."

The young woman returned to the dining-room and gave a final glance at the preparations.

"He's a pretty good sort, my august lover." Justine started in surprise.

"August! Is that a new one?"

Susy d'Orsel could hardly repress a smile.

"Mind your own business. What time is it?"

"A quarter to twelve, Madame." And as the girl started to leave the room she ventured:

"I hope M. August won't forget me, to-morrow morning."

"Why, you little idiot, his name isn't August, it's Frederick-Christian! You have about as much sense as an oyster!"

The maid looked so crestfallen at this that Susy added, good-naturedly:

"That's all right, Justine, A Happy New Year anyway, and don't worry. And now get out; His Majesty wants nobody about but me this evening."

Susy d'Orsel, in spite of her physical charms, had found life hard during the earlier years of her career. She had become a mediocre actress merely for the sake of having some profession, and had frequented the night restaurants in quest of a wealthy lover. It was only after a long delay that fortune had smiled upon her, and she had arrived at the enviable position of being the mistress of a King.

Frederick-Christian II, since the death of his father three years previously, reigned over the destinies of the Kingdom of Hesse-Weimar. Young and thoroughly Parisian in his tastes, he felt terribly bored in his middle-class capital and sought every opportunity of going, incognito, to have a little fun in Paris. During each visit he never failed to call upon Susy d'Orsel, and by degrees, coming under the sway of her charms, he made her a sort of official mistress, an honor which greatly redounded to her glory and popularity.

He had installed her in a dainty little apartment in the Rue de Monceau. It was on the third floor and charmingly furnished. In fact, he was in the habit of declaring that his Queen Hedwige, despite all her wealth, was unable to make her apartment half so gracious and comfortable.

Thus it was that Susy d'Orsel waited patiently for the arrival of her royal lover, who had telephoned her he would be with her on the night of December the thirty-first.

The official residence of the King while in Paris was the Royal Palace Hotel, and although in strict incognito, he rarely spent the whole night out. But he intended to make the last night of the year an exception to this rule. As became a gallant gentleman, he had himself seen to the ordering of the supper, and a procession of waiters from the first restaurants of Paris had been busy all the afternoon preparing for the feast.

Suddenly a discreet ring at the bell startled Susy d'Orsel.

"That's queer, I didn't expect the King until one o'clock!" she exclaimed.

She opened the door and saw a young girl standing on the landing.

"Oh, it's you, Mademoiselle Pascal! What are you coming at this hour for?"

"Excuse me, Madame, for troubling you, but I've brought your lace negligée. It took me quite a time to finish, and I thought you'd probably like it as soon as possible."

"Oh, I thought it had already come. I'm very glad you brought it. There would have been a fine row if it hadn't been ready for me to wear this evening."

Susy d'Orsel took the dressmaker into her bedroom and turned on the electric lights. The gown was then unwrapped and displayed. It was of mousseline de soie, trimmed with English point.

Susy examined it with the eye of a connoisseur and then nodded her head.

"It's fine, my girl, you have the fingers of a fairy, but it must put your eyes out."

"It is very hard, Madame, especially working by artificial light, and in winter the days are so short and the work very heavy. That is why I came to you at this late hour."

Susy smiled.

"Late hour! Why the evening is just beginning for me."

"Our lives are very different, Madame."

"That's right, I begin when you stop, and if your work is hard, mine isn't always agreeable."

The two women laughed and then Susy took off her wrapper and put on the new negligée.

"My royal lover is coming this evening."

"Yes, I know," answered Marie Pascal. "Your table looks very pretty."

"You might make me a lace table cloth. We'll talk about it some other time, not this evening; besides, I can't be too extravagant."

The dressmaker took her leave a few moments later and made her way with care in the semi-obscurity down the three flights of stairs.

Marie Pascal was a young girl in the early twenties, fair-haired, blue-eyed and with a graceful figure. Modishly but neatly dressed, she had a reputation in the neighborhood as a model of discretion and virtue.

She worked ceaselessly and being clever with her fingers, she had succeeded in building up so good a trade in the rich and elegant Monceau quarter, that in the busy season she was obliged to hire one or two workwomen to help her.

As she was crossing the court to go to her own room, a voice called her from the porter's lodge.

"Marie Pascal, look here a moment."

A fat woman dressed in her best opened the door of her room which was lit by one flaring gas jet.

Marie Pascal, in spite of her natural kindliness, could scarcely repress a smile.

Madame Ceiron, the concièrge, or, as she was popularly called, "Mother Citron," certainly presented a fantastic appearance.

She was large, shapeless, common, and good-natured. Behind her glasses, her eyes snapped with perpetual sharp humor. She had a mass of gray hair that curled round her wrinkled face, which, with a last remnant of coquetry, she made up outrageously. Her hands and feet were enormous, disproportionate to her figure, although she was well above middle height. She invariably wore mittens while doing the housework.

Mother Citron, however, did very little work; she left that to a subordinate who, for a modest wage, attended to her business and left her free to go out morning, noon and night. She now questioned Marie Pascal with considerable curiosity, and the young girl explained her late errand to deliver the gown to Susy d'Orsel.

"Come in and have a cup of coffee, Mam'zelle Pascal," urged the old woman, as she set out two cups and filled them from a coffee pot on the stove.

Marie Pascal at first refused, but Mother Citron was so insistent that she ended by accepting the invitation. Besides, she felt very grateful to Madame Ceiron for having recommended her to the proprietor of the house, the Marquis de Sérac, an old bachelor who lived on the first floor.

The Marquis had used his good offices to obtain for her an order for laces from the King of Hesse-Weimar. Mother Citron showed a kindly interest in this enterprise.

"Well, did you see the King?"

Marie Pascal hesitated:

"I saw him and I didn't see him."

"Tell me all about it, my dear. Is the lover of our lady upstairs a good-looking man?"

"It's hard to say. So far as I could judge, he seemed to be very handsome. You see, it was like this. After waiting in the lobby of the Royal Palace Hotel for about an hour, I was shown into a large drawing-room; a sort of footman in knee breeches took my laces into the adjoining room where the King was walking up and down. I just caught a glimpse of him from time to time."

"What did he do then?"

"I don't know. He must have liked my laces for he gave me a large order. He didn't seem to pay much attention to them; he picked out three of the samples I sent in and what seemed queer, he also ordered some imitations of them."

The concièrge smiled knowingly.

"I expect the imitations were for his lawful wife, and the real ones for his little friend. Men are all alike. Another cup of coffee?"

"Oh, no, thanks."

"Well, I won't insist; each one to his taste. The life Susy d'Orsel leads wouldn't suit you. And the amount of champagne she gets through!"

"No, I shouldn't care much about that."

"All the same, there's something to be said for it. She has a first-rate position since she got the King … and I get first-rate tips! Take to-night, for instance; I'll bet they'll be carrying on till pretty near dawn. It upsets my habits, but I can't complain. I'll probably get a good New Year's present in the morning."

"Well, as it's very late for me, I'll go up to bed."

"Go ahead, my dear, don't let me keep you."

Marie Pascal had reached the stairs when she turned back.

"Oh, Madame Ceiron, when can I thank the Marquis de Sérac for his kindness in introducing me to Frederick-Christian?"

"No hurry, my child, the Marquis has gone to the country to spend the New Year's day with his relations and he won't be back before next week."

Marie Pascal climbed the stairs to her room on the sixth floor and the concièrge returned to her quarters and settled herself in an armchair.

CHAPTER III
THE TRAGEDY OF THE RUE DE MONCEAU

Susy d'Orsel, tired of waiting for her royal lover, was sound asleep before the fire in her bedroom. Suddenly she was awakened by a loud noise. Still half asleep, she sat up listening. The sounds came from the stairs. Mechanically Susy glanced at the clock, which marked the quarter after three.

"I'll bet it's him, but how late he is!"

As the sounds drew nearer, she added:

"He must be as drunk as a lord! After all, Kings are no better than other men."

She quickly passed to the outer door and listened.

"Why, it sounds as if there were two of them!"

A key fumbled in the lock, then the owner of it apparently gave up the task as hopeless and began ringing the bell.

Susy opened the door and Frederick-Christian staggered in followed by a man who was a total stranger to her.

The latter, bowing in a correct and respectful manner, carried himself with dignity.

The King bubbled over with laughter and leaned on the shoulder of his lady-love.

"Take off your overcoat," she said, at length, and while he was attempting to obey her, she whispered:

"If your Maj..."

Before she could finish the sentence the King put his hand over her mouth.

"My ... my ... my dear Susy ... I'm very fond of you ... but don't begin by saying stupid things.... I am here ... incog ... incognito. Call me your little Cri-Cri, Susy...."

"My dear," she replied, "introduce me to your friend."

"Eh," cried the King, "if I'm not forgetting the most elementary obligations of the protocol; but after fourteen whiskeys, and good whiskey, too, though I've better here.... Susy don't drink any, she prefers gooseberry syrup ... queer taste, isn't it?"

Susy saw the conversation was getting away from the point, so repeated her request:

"Introduce me to your friend."

Frederick-Christian glanced at his companion and then burst out laughing:

"What is your name, anyway?"

Fandor did not need to ask that question of the King. The moment he had set eyes on him in Raxim's he recognized in the sturdy tippler his Majesty Frederick-Christian II, King of Hesse-Weimar, on one of his periodic sprees. It was this fact which had made him break his rule and indulge freely himself.

With a serious air he explained:

"Sum fides Achates!"

"What's that?" cried the King.

"Exactly."

Susy d'Orsel now thought both men were equally drunk. She fancied they were having fun with her.

"You know I don't want English spoken here," she said drily.

The King took his mistress round the waist and drew her to him.

"Now don't get angry, my dear, it's only our fun, and besides it's not English, it's Latin ... bonus ... Latinus ... ancestribus ... the good Latin of our ancestors!... the Latin of the Kitchen! Cuisinus ... autobus ... understand?"

Turning to the journalist he stretched out his hand:

"Well, my old friend Achates, I'm jolly glad to meet you."

"Achates isn't a real name," cried Susy, still suspicious.

"Achates," explained Fandor, "is an individual belonging to antiquity who became famous in his faithful friendship for his companion and friend, the well-known globe-trotter, Æneas."

"Come and sit down," shouted the King, as he rapped on the table with a bottle of champagne.

"Hurry up, Susy, a plate and glass for my old friend, whose name I don't know ...because, you see, he's no more Achates than I am."

"Oh, no, Madame," Fandor hastened to say, "I couldn't think of putting you to the trouble, besides spoiling the effect of your charming table. In fact, I am going home in a few moments."

"Not on your life," shouted the King, "you'll stay to the very end."

"Well, then, a glass of champagne, that's all I'll take."

By degrees Susy had become reassured in regard to the young man. Although slightly drunk, his polite manner and good form pleased her. She took her place on the divan beside the King. Fandor sat opposite them and lighted a cigarette.

Suddenly Susy rose from the table.

"Where are you going?" demanded the King.

"I'll be back in a moment ...something must be open. I feel a draught on my legs."

"Why not show us your legs!" cried Frederick-Christian, and turning to the journalist added: "She's built like a statue ...a little marvel."

Susy returned.

"I knew it! The hall door was open. I hope nobody has got in."

The King laughed at the idea.

"If anyone did, let him come and join us, the more the merrier."

"I thought I heard a noise," continued Susy, but the King made her sit down again beside him and the supper went on.

As she drank glass after glass of wine, she became more and more amiable toward Fandor. And since the King paid little attention to her caresses, she began a flirtation with the journalist in order to pique him.

This brought a frown from the royal lover, and Susy amused herself between the two men until supper ended and they all adjourned to her boudoir.

Fandor, who had now become more sober, decided it was time to take his leave.

"Suppose you both come and lunch with me to-morrow, will you?" he asked. To this they agreed and it was finally arranged that Fandor should call and pick them up at one o'clock the following day.

The journalist felt his way downstairs in the semi-darkness and was just about to ask the concièrge to let him out when he was startled by seeing a heavy form fall with a thud onto the ground of the inner court.

With a gasp of alarm the young man rushed forward and quickly realized that he was in the presence of a terrible tragedy.

Lying on the ground, inert, was the body of Susy d'Orsel.

The unfortunate girl had fallen from the third floor.

Without hesitating, he lifted the body and finding no sign of life, cried loudly for help.

But the entire house was asleep.

What was to be done?

Immediate action was necessary. After a moment's pause, he decided to take the unfortunate girl back to her own apartment. Arrived at the door, he found it locked on the inside. After ringing for some time, it was opened finally by the King. At the sight of Susy apparently lifeless, her head hanging backward, the King staggered to the wall.

He wanted to ask a question, but the words stuck in his throat.

Fandor entered the bedroom and laying Susy down attempted to undo her corset.

"Vinegar and some water," he ordered.

The King between his drunkenness and his alarm was quite useless, and the journalist, after applying a mirror to the girl's nostrils and lips, with a gesture of despair exclaimed:

"Good God, she is dead!"

However, being unwilling to risk his own judgment, he started to the door to seek aid.

At this moment a violent knocking began and a voice from the hall cried out:

"What's the matter? Is anyone hurt? I'm the concièrge."

"The concièrge! Then, for Heaven's sake, Madame, get a doctor. Mademoiselle d'Orsel has killed herself, or at least she is very badly injured."

The words were scarcely out of Fandor's mouth when the rapidly disappearing footsteps of the concièrge were heard clattering downstairs. Frederick-Christian, in a dazed condition, stood in the dining-room, mechanically drinking a liqueur.

"Look here, what does this mean?" cried Fandor.

The King looked at him with intense stupefaction, trying, it seemed, to co-ordinate his faculties. Then, with a greater calmness than in his condition seemed possible, he replied:

"Why, I haven't the least idea."

"But ... what have you done since I left you? You were both seated side by side on the sofa. How did Susy d'Orsel come to fall out of the window? What have you done?"

"I don't know. I didn't budge from the sofa until you rang the bell."

"But ... Susy!"

"She left me for a moment. I thought she had gone to see you out."

"That's impossible ... she didn't leave you ... it's you who ... for God's sake, explain!... It's too serious a business."

The King seemed unable to take in the situation. Fandor determined to try a shock. Going close to him he spoke in a low voice:

"I beg your Majesty to tell me."

This had an immediate effect. The King staggered back and stared, wide-eyed.

"I ... I don't understand."

"Yes," insisted Fandor, "your Majesty does understand. You know that I am aware in whose presence I am standing. You are Frederick-Christian II, King of Hesse-Weimar... and I, your Majesty, am Jerome Fandor, reporter on *La Capitale* ... a journalist."

The King did not appear to attach much importance to Fandor's words. Peaceably, without haste, he put on his overcoat and hat. Then, picking up his cane, he moved toward the door.

"Here! what are you doing?"

"I'm going."

"You can't."

"Yes, I can; it's all right, don't worry, I'll arrange matters."

The King appeared so calmly confident that Fandor stood dumbfounded.

Here certainly was an individual out of the common! The journalist had seen many strange happenings in his adventurous career, but never had he come across such an amazing situation. For now he had no doubt of the guilt of the King. What, however, could have been the motive of such odious savagery? Was it possible he had taken seriously the innocent flirtation between Susy and himself? Had the King taken vengeance upon his mistress in a moment of jealous insanity?

No, that was out of the question.

In spite of his intoxication, Frederick-Christian seemed to be a man of normal temperament, and of a kindly disposition. His face betrayed none of the characteristics of the drink-maddened.

The young man was about to question Frederick-Christian further when the hall door bell rang sharply.

Fandor quickly opened the door and let in two policemen.

"Is it here the tragedy took place?"

"What! You know already?"

"The concièrge notified us, Monsieur."

Then turning to his companion:

"See that no one gets out."

"But I've sent for a doctor.... I must go and find one," cried Fandor.

"That has already been attended to. We are here to ascertain the facts, to make arrests. Where is the victim of the crime?"

As Fandor took the officer into the bedroom he expected at every moment to hear some exclamation at the discovery of the King. But the latter had mysteriously disappeared.

The officer surveyed the body of the young woman and seemed in doubt how to begin his interrogatory. Suddenly his attention was diverted to the vestibule, where whispering was going on.

Both men quickly returned to the hall door and Fandor overheard the final words of a third person who had entered the room, evidently the concièrge. She was saying:

"It must be 'him' ... only treat him politely ... he isn't like an ordinary..."

Upon seeing the journalist the old woman stopped abruptly and made him a deep bow.

"Ah, it's you, Madame," cried Fandor, "well, have you brought a doctor?"

"We're looking for one, Monsieur," replied the old woman, "but to-night they seem to be all out enjoying themselves."

One of the officers turned to Fandor and spoke with evident embarrassment.

"It might be better if Monsieur would tell us exactly what happened. On account of possible annoyances ... besides, the business is too important ... and then the Government..."

Fandor explained briefly all he knew. He was careful not to mention the King by name, leaving it to his Majesty to disclose his own identity when the time came.

"Then Monsieur means to say that a third person was present?" one of the officers asked.

"Of course!" replied Fandor.

"And where is this third person?"

The officer looked decidedly skeptical and the journalist began to grow uneasy.

"He was here with me just now; probably he's in one of the other rooms. Why don't you search?"

But the search disclosed nobody.

What on earth had become of the King? thought Fandor. He couldn't have jumped out of the window. The servant's staircase came into his mind, but the door to that he found locked.

"It is useless for Monsieur to say more; kindly come with us to the police station."

"After all, Monsieur was alone with the little lady," added the concièrge.

Fandor went rapidly to the dining-room. He would show the three places at the table. But suddenly he remembered his refusal to take a plate. There were only two places laid.

The two officers now held him gently by each arm and began to walk away with him.

"Don't make any noise, please," they urged, "we must avoid all scandal."

Without quite understanding what was happening, Fandor obeyed.

CHAPTER IV
WHO DO THEY THINK I AM?

The first faint light of dawn was filtering through the dusty windows of the police station.

Sergeant Masson, pushing aside the game of dominoes he had been playing with his subordinate, declared:

"I must go and see the chief."

"At his house?" demanded the other in a tone of alarm.

"Yes; after all, if I catch it for waking him that won't be so bad as having him come here at ten."

The sergeant rose and stretched himself. He had entire charge of the Station and was responsible for all arrests. As a rule he felt himself equal to the task, but this time the tragedy of the Rue Monceau and the peculiar circumstances surrounding it seemed too much of a burden to bear alone.

Ought he to have arrested the individual now at the Station? Had he been sufficiently tactful? What was to be done now?

"Yes, I'm going to see the chief," he repeated, "besides, I shan't be gone long. Anything that 'he' asks for let him have, you understand?"

It was about five-thirty, and the sky threatened snow. The air was fresh and not too cold. A few milk carts were the only vehicles in the streets. Porters were busy brushing off the sidewalks. Paris was making her toilette. Sergeant Masson stopped at a small house in a quiet street and mounted to the third floor. There he hesitated. The wife of the chief was known for her sharp temper. However, there was nothing to be done but ring, and this he did in a timid manner.

In a few moments he heard the door-chain withdrawn, and a woman's voice cried:

"Who is there?"

"It is I, Madame, Sergeant Masson."

"Well, what do you want?"

"The chief is wanted at the Station right away."

At these words the door opened wide and the woman stood revealed. She was about forty, dressed in her wrapper and with her hair still in curl papers.

"Louis must go to the Station?" she demanded.

"Yes, Madame, an arrest has been made..."

"He must go to the Station?" she repeated in a menacing tone.

Sergeant Masson retreated to the landing. He simply nodded his head.

"But he *is* there! He told me he was! Ah, I see how it is!...He's been lying again. He's been running after women...all right, he'll pay for it when he gets home!"

The door shut with a bang and the lady disappeared.

"What an idiot I've been," muttered the discomfited sergeant. "I ought to have known better. Of course he's not with his wife, he's with his mistress!"

Several minutes later he reached another apartment in a neighboring street.

This time he had no misgivings and congratulated himself upon his professional cleverness in tracking his man down.

The same performance was gone through. A ring at the bell brought an answer to the door.

"Who is there?" said a man's voice.

"It is I ... Sergeant Masson."

The door was opened and a young man stood in the hall. He was about thirty and wore an undershirt and drawers.

"Well, Sergeant!"

The sergeant shrank back; he would have been glad if he could have disappeared in the walls. The chief's secretary stood before him.

"I was ...was looking ..." he stammered.

The secretary interrupted with a smile.

"No, he's not here. In fact, we are rarely found together."

Then putting a hand on the sergeant's shoulder:

"As gentleman to gentleman, I count on your discretion."

The door shut softly and the sergeant turned sadly and went back to the Station, pondering over the personal annoyance this general post at night occasioned him.

He was greeted on his return by a few sharp words.

"Ah, there you are, Masson!...At last!...An event of the first importance occurs, an amazing scandal breaks out and you desert your post....It's always the way if I'm not here to look after things. I shall have to report you, you know. Where have you been?"

The speaker was a man still quite young, who wore the ribbon of the Legion of Honor. It was the chief himself. On the way home from some late party he had dropped into the Station out of simple curiosity.

Was he awake or was he dreaming?

Fandor felt stiff all over, his head was heavy and his mind a blank....And then came a thirst, a devouring, insatiable thirst.

Where he was and how he had arrived there were things past his comprehension.

So far as the feeble light permitted, he made out the room to contain the furnishings of an office, and by degrees, as his mind cleared, he recalled with a start his arrest.

He was at the police station.

But why in this particular room? The walls were hung with sporting prints. Bookshelves, a comfortable sofa, upon which he had spent the night, all these indicated nothing less than the private office of the chief.

And then he recalled with what consideration he had been conducted hither. Evidently they took him for an intimate friend of the King. Nevertheless, he was under arrest for murder, or at least as an accomplice to a murder.

"After all," he thought, "the truth will come to light, they'll capture the murderer and my innocence will be established.

"Besides, didn't the King promise to see me through. Probably before this he has already taken steps for my release."

He then decided to call out:

"Is there anyone here?"

Scarcely had Fandor spoken when a man entered, who, after a profound bow to the journalist, drew the curtains apart.

"You are awake, Monsieur?"

Fandor was amazed. What charming manners the police had!

"Oh, yes, I'm awake, but I feel stiff all over."

"That is easily understood, and I hope you will pardon ...You see, I didn't happen to be at the station ...and when I got here ...why, I didn't like to wake you."

"They take me for a friend of the King of Hesse-Weimar," thought Fandor.

"You did perfectly right, Monsieur..."

"M. Perrajas, District Commissioner of Police ...and the circumstances being such ...the unfortunate circumstances ...I imagine it was better that you did not return immediately to your apartment ...in fact, I have given the necessary orders and in a few moments ...the time to get a carriage ...I can, of course, rely upon the discretion of my men who, besides, are ignorant of..."

"Oh, that's all right."

Fandor replied in a non-committal tone. It would be wiser to avoid any compromising admission. A carriage! — what carriage, doubtless the Black Maria to take him to prison. And what did he mean by 'the discretion of his men?'

"Well," thought Fandor, "he can count upon me. I shan't publish anything yet. And after all, it's going to be very hard for me to prove my innocence. Since I must rely on the King getting me out of this hole, it would be very foolish of me to give him away."

"Besides," continued the officer, "I have had the concièrge warned; she has received the most positive orders ... and no reporter will be allowed to get hold of..."

The officer became confused in his explanation.

"The incidents of last night," added Fandor.

A knock at the door and Sergeant Masson entered.

"The coupé is ready."

"Very well, Sergeant."

Fandor rose and was about to put on his overcoat, but the man darted forward and helped him on with it.

"Do you wish me to come with you, Monsieur, or would you prefer to return alone?"

"Oh, alone, thanks, don't trouble yourself."

The door was opened wide by the polite officer and Fandor passed through the main hall of the Station, where everyone rose and bowed. Getting into his carriage, he was disagreeably surprised to see an individual who appeared to be a plain clothes man sitting on the seat. In addition a police cyclist fell in behind the carriage as escort.

"Where the devil are they going to take me?" he wondered.

To his intense surprise, they stopped ten minutes later at the Royal Palace, the most luxurious hotel in Paris.

With infinite deference he was then conducted to the elevator and taken to the first floor.

"Well, this lets me out," thought Fandor. "Evidently the King has sent for me ... in a few minutes I shall be free ... what a piece of luck!"

He was shown into a sumptuous apartment and there left to his own devices.

"Wonder what's become of Frederick-Christian," he muttered, after a wait of twenty minutes. "It's worse than being at the dentist's."

As the room was very warm, Fandor removed his overcoat and began an investigation of his surroundings. Upon a table lay several illustrated papers and picking one up he seated himself comfortably in an armchair and began to read.

Some minutes later a Major-domo entered the room with much ceremony and silently presented him with a card. This turned out to be a menu.

"Well, they're not going to let me starve anyway," he thought, "and as long as the King has asked me to breakfast, I'll accept his invitation."

Choosing several dishes at random, he returned the menu, and the man, bowing deeply, inquired:

"Where shall we serve breakfast? In the boudoir?"

"Yes, in the boudoir."

The bow ended the interview and Fandor was once more left alone. But not for long. Close upon the heels of the first, a second man entered and handed the journalist a telegram and withdrew.

"Ah, now I shall get some explanation of all this mystery! This should come from the King.... Has he got my name?... No!... the Duke of Haworth ... evidently the name of the individual I am supposed to represent."

Fandor tore open the telegram and then stared in surprise. Not one word of it could he make out. It was in cipher!

"Why the deuce was this given to me!... what does the whole thing mean? Is it possible they take me for...."

CHAPTER V
BY THE SINGING FOUNTAINS

Paris rises very late indeed on New Year's Day. The night before is given up to family reunions, supper parties and every kind of jollification. So the year begins with a much needed rest. The glitter and racket of the streets gives place to a death-like stillness. Shops are shut and the cafés are empty. Paris sleeps. There is an exception to this rule: Certain unfortunate individuals are obliged to rise at day-break, don their best clothes, their uniforms and make their way to the four corners of the town to pay ceremonial calls.

These are the Government officials representing the army, the magistracy, the parliament, the municipality — all must pay their respects to their chiefs. For this hardship they receive little sympathy, as it is generally understood that while they have to work hard on New Year's Day, they do nothing for the rest of the year.

The somnolence of Paris, however, only extends until noon. At that hour life begins again. It is luncheon time.

This New Year's Day differed in no wise from others, and during the afternoon the streets were thronged with people.

A pale sun showed in the gray winter sky and the crowd seemed to be converging toward the Place de la Concorde. Suddenly the blare of a brass band on the Rue Royale brought curious heads to the windows.

A procession headed by a vari-colored banner was marching toward the banks of the Seine. The participants wore a mauve uniform with gold trimmings and upon the banner was inscribed in huge letters:

LA CAPITALE
THE GREAT EVENING PAPER

With some difficulty the musicians reached the Obelisk and at the foot of the monument they formed a circle, while at a distance the crowd awaited developments.

In the front rank two young women were standing.

One of them seemed to be greatly amused at the gratuitous entertainment, the other appeared preoccupied and depressed.

"Come, Marie Pascal, don't be so absent-minded. You look as if you were at a funeral."

The other, a workgirl, tried to smile and gave a deep sigh.

"I'm sorry, Mademoiselle Rose, to be out of sorts, but I feel very upset."

Two police officers tried to force their way to the musicians and after some difficulty they succeeded in arresting the flute and the trombone players.

This act of brutality occasioned some commotion and the crowd began to murmur.

The employés of *La Capitale* now brought up several handcarts and improvised a sort of platform. Gentlemen in frock coats then appeared on the scene and gathered round it. One or two were recognized and pointed out by the crowd.

"There's M. Dupont, the deputy and director of *La Capitale*."

A red-faced young man with turned up moustaches was pronounced to be M. de Panteloup, the general manager of the paper.

As a matter of fact, those who read *La Capitale* had been advised through its columns that an attempt would be made to solve the mystery of the Singing Fountains, which had intrigued Paris for so many weeks. A small army of newsboys offered the paper for sale during the ceremony. Marie Pascal bought a copy and read it eagerly.

"They haven't a word about the affair yet," she cried.

At that moment the powerful voice of M. de Panteloup was heard:

"You are now going to hear an interesting speech by the celebrated archivist and paleographer, M. Anastasius Baringouin, who, better than anyone else, can explain to you the strange enigma of the Singing Fountains."

An immense shout of laughter greeted the orator as he mounted the steps to the stage. He was an old man, very wrinkled and shaky, wearing a high hat much too large for his head. He was vainly trying to settle his glasses upon a very red nose. In a thin, sharp voice, he began:

"The phenomenon of the Singing Fountains is not, as might be supposed, wholly unexpected. Similar occurrences have already been noted and date back to remote antiquity. Formerly a stone statue was erected in the outskirts of the town of Thebes to the memory of Memnon. When the beams of the rising sun struck it, harmonious sounds were heard to issue from it. At first this peculiarity was attributed to some form of trickery, a secret spring or a hidden keyboard. But upon further research, it was demonstrated that the sounds arose from purely physical and natural causes."

The crowd which hitherto had listened in silence to the orator now began to show signs of impatience.

"What the dickens is he gassing about?" shouted some one in the street.

As the savant paid no attention to these signs the band struck up a military march. Finally when order was re-established M. Panteloup himself mounted the platform.

"This fountain, ladies and gentlemen," he began in a powerful voice, "was built in 1836 at a cost of a million and a half francs. In the twenty-four hours its output is 6,716 cubic yards of water. It is composed, as you can see, of a basin of polished stone, decorated by six tritons and nereids, each holding a fish in its mouth from which the water flows out. Thus far there is nothing unusual and it is therefore with justifiable surprise that we discover the fact that at certain moments these fountains actually sing. Are we in the presence of a phenomenon similar to that recalled just now by M. Anastasius Baringouin? Are we, at the beginning of the twentieth century — the century of Science and Precision — victims of hallucination or sorcery? This, ladies and gentlemen, is what we are about to investigate, and we will begin by consulting the celebrated clairvoyant, Madame Gabrielle de Smyrne."

A murmur of approbation greeted the pretty prophetess as she appeared, but at the same moment a police officer followed by fifteen men pushed his way to the foot of the platform and ordered M. Panteloup to cease attracting a crowd. The latter, however, was equal to the occasion. After lifting his hand for silence he shouted the famous cry:

"We are here by the will of the people, we shall not go away except by force."

The crowd cheered, and with the voices mingled the barking of dogs.

"Ladies and gentlemen," continued M. Panteloup, "you hear the wonderful police dogs of Neuilly, Turk and Bellone. They are coming to help us to scent out the mystery."

This was to be the termination of the ceremony, but an unlooked for addition to the program appeared in the person of one of those Parisian "Natural Men" or "Primitive Men."

He was a very old, long-bearded man and wore a white robe. He went by the name of Ouaouaoua, and his portrait had been published in all city papers. A hush came over the crowd and then in the silence a vague metallic murmur was heard above the splash of the water.

This time there was no mistake. The Fountains were singing.

Thousands of witnesses were present and could testify to that fact.

The crowd at once associated the arrival of Ouaouaoua with the music from the Fountains, and he was acclaimed the hero of the occasion.

M. de Panteloup, seized with a happy inspiration, shook hands with Ouaouaoua and pinned on his white robe the gold medal of *La Capitale*.

Proceedings were, however, summarily brought to a stop at this point. The prefect of the police drove up and his men scattered the crowd in all directions.

Ten minutes after the Place de la Concorde had assumed its usual aspect and the tritons and nereids continued to pour out their 6,716 cubic yards of water every twenty-four hours.

CHAPTER VI
THE INVESTIGATION BEGINS

M. Vicart, sub-director of the Police Department, was in an execrable humor.

In all his long career such a thing had never happened before. In spite of the established rule, he had been deprived of his New Year holiday, which he usually spent in visits to governmental officials capable of influencing his advancement.

He had been ordered to his office. His morning had been spent in endless discussions with M. Annion, his director. Numerous telegrams, interviews, work of all kinds instead of his customary rest. Besides, he had received from his friends only 318 visiting cards instead of 384, last year's number. It was most annoying. He was engaged in recounting his cards when a clerk announced the visit of detective Juve.

"Send him in at once."

In a few moments Juve entered.

Juve had not changed. In spite of his forty-odd years, he was still young looking, active, persevering and daring.

For some time past he had been left very much to his own devices in his tracking of the elusive Fantômas, and he was rarely called in to assist in the pursuit of other criminals. Therefore he realized that it was an affair of the very first importance which called for his presence in M. Vicart's office.

The detective found M. Vicart seated at his desk in the badly lighted room.

"My dear Juve, you are probably surprised at being sent for to-day."

"A little ... yes."

"Well, you probably know that the King of Hesse-Weimar, Frederick-Christian II, has been staying incognito in Paris?"

Juve nodded. He did not think it necessary to mention the incident that had occasioned this visit.[1]

"Now, Christian II has, or rather had, a mistress, Susy d'Orsel, a demi-mondaine. Were you aware of that?"

"No, what of it?"

"This woman has been murdered ... or rather ... has not been murdered ... you understand, Juve, has not been murdered."

"Has not been murdered, very well!"

"Now, this woman who has not been murdered threw herself out of the window last night at three o'clock; in a word, she committed suicide, at the precise moment when Frederick-Christian was taking supper with her ... you grasp my meaning?"

"No, I don't. What are you trying to get at?"

"Why, it's as clear as day, Juve ... the scandal! especially as the local magistrate had the stupidity to arrest the King."

"The King has been arrested ... I don't understand! Then it wasn't suicide?"

"That is what must be established."

"And I am to take charge of the investigation?"

"I put it in your hands."

When M. Vicart had explained the circumstances of the case, Juve summed up:

"In a word, Frederick-Christian II went to see his mistress last night, she threw herself out of the window, the King was arrested for murder; he put in a denial, claiming that a third person was present, this third person escaped, an inadmissible hypothesis, since nobody saw him and the door to the servant's staircase was locked ... this morning the King was set at liberty, and we have now to find out whether a crime was really committed or whether it was a case of suicide.... Is that it?"

"That is it! But you're going ahead pretty fast. You don't realize, Juve, the seriousness of the supposition you formulate so freely.... You must know whether it's murder or suicide! Of course! Of course!...but you are too precise....A King a murderer ...that isn't possible. There would be terrible diplomatic complications....It's a case of suicide....Susy d'Orsel committed suicide beyond a doubt."

Juve smiled slightly.

"That has to be proved, hasn't it?"

"Certainly it must be proved. The accident happened at number 247 Rue de Monceau. Go there, question the concierge ... the only witness....In a word, bring us the proof of suicide in written form. We can then send a report to the press and stifle the threatened scandal."

Juve rose.

"I will begin an immediate investigation," he replied, smiling, "and M. Vicart, you may depend upon me to use all means in my power to clear up the affair ...entirely and impartially."

When Juve had gone, M. Vicart realized a sense of extreme uneasiness.

"Impartially!... the deuce!"

Hurriedly he left his office and made his way through the halls to his chief, M. Annion. His first care must be to cover his own responsibility in the matter.

M. Annion, cold and impassive, listened to his recital in silence and then broke out:

"You have committed a blunder, M. Vicart. I told you this morning to put a detective on the case who would bring us a report along the lines that we desire. I pointed out to you the gravity of the situation."

"But ..." protested M. Vicart.

"Let me finish....I thought I had made myself quite clear on that point and now, you actually give the commission to Juve!"

"Exactly, Monsieur! I gave Juve the commission because he is our most expert detective."

"That I don't deny, and therefore Juve is certain to discover the truth! It is an unpardonable blunder."

At this moment a clerk entered with a telegram. M. Annion opened it quickly and read it.

"Ah! this is enough to bring about the fall of the Ministry. Listen!"

"The Minister of Hesse-Weimar to the Secretary of the Interior, Place Beauvau, Paris — Numerous telegrams addressed to his Majesty the King of Hesse-Weimar, at present staying incognito at the Royal Palace Hotel, Avenue des Champs Elysées, remain unanswered, in spite of their extreme urgency. The Minister of Hesse-Weimar begs the Secretary of the Interior of France to kindly make inquiries and to send him the assurance that his Majesty the King of Hesse-Weimar is in possession of these diplomatic telegrams."

M. Annion burst out.

"There now! Pretty soon they'll be accusing us of intercepting the telegrams ...Frederick-Christian doesn't answer! How can I help that! I suppose he's weeping over the death of his mistress. And now that fellow Juve has taken a hand in it! I tell you. Monsieur Vicart, we're in a nice fix!"

While M. Annion was unburdening his mind to M. Vicart, Juve left the Ministry whistling a march, and hailed a cab to take him to the Rue Monceau.

He quite understood what was required of him, but his professional pride, his independence and his innate honesty of purpose determined him to ferret out the truth regardless of consequences.

As a matter of fact, the presence of the King in Paris was, in part, to render a service to Juve himself.[2]

If, therefore, the hypothesis of suicide could be verified, Juve would be able to be of use to the King; if, on the other hand, it had to be rejected, his report would prove that fact.

On arriving at the Rue de Monceau, Juve went straight to the concierge's office and having shown his badge, began to question her:

"Tell me, Madame Ceiron, did you see the King when he came to pay his visit to his mistress?"

"No, Monsieur. I saw nothing at all. I was in bed ... the bell rang, I opened the door ... the King called out as usual, 'the Duke of Haworth' — it's the name he goes by — and then he went upstairs, but I didn't see him."

"Was he alone?"

"Ah, that's what everyone asks me! Of course he was alone ... the proof being that when they went up and found poor Mlle. Susy, nobody else was there, so..."

Juve interrupted:

"All right. Now, tell me, did Mlle. Susy d'Orsel expect any other visitor? Any friend?"

"Nobody that I knew of ... at least that's what she said to her lace-maker — one of my tenants ... a very good young girl, Mlle. Marie Pascal — She said like this — 'I'm expecting my lover,' but she mentioned nobody else."

"And this Marie Pascal is the last person who saw Susy d'Orsel alive, excepting, of course, the King? The servants had gone to bed?"

"Oh, Monsieur, the maid wasn't there. Justine came down about eleven, she said good-night to me as she went by ... while Marie Pascal didn't go up before eleven-thirty or a quarter to twelve."

"Very well, I'll see Mlle. Pascal later. Another question, Mme. Ceiron: did any of your tenants leave the house after the crime ... I mean after the death?"

"No, Monsieur."

"Mlle. Susy d'Orsel's apartment is reached by two staircases. Do you know if the door to the one used by the servants was locked?"

"That I can't tell you, Monsieur, all I know is that Justine generally locked it when she went out."

"And while you were away hunting the doctor and the police, did you leave the door of the house open?"

"Ah, no, Monsieur, to begin with, I didn't go out. I have a telephone in my room, besides I never leave the door open."

"Is Justine in her room now?"

"No, I have the key, which means that she's out ... she's probably looking after funeral arrangements of the poor young girl."

"Mlle. d'Orsel had no relations?"

"I don't think so, Monsieur."

"Is Marie Pascal in?"

"Yes ... sixth floor to the right at the end of the hall."

"Then I will go up and see her. Thanks very much for your information, Madame."

"You're very welcome, Monsieur. Ah, this wretched business isn't going to help the house. I still have two apartments unrented."

Juve did not wait to hear the good woman's lamentations but hurriedly climbed the flights of stairs and knocked on the door indicated.

It was opened by a young girl.

"Mademoiselle Marie Pascal?"

"Yes, Monsieur."

"Can I see you for a couple of minutes? I am a detective and have charge of investigating the death of Mlle. d'Orsel."

Mlle. Pascal led the way into her modest room, which was bright and sunny with a flowered paper on the walls, potted plants and a bird-cage. She then began a recital of the interview she had had with Susy. This threw no fresh light upon the case and at the end, Juve replied:

"To sum it up, Mademoiselle, you know only one thing, that Mlle. d'Orsel was waiting for her lover, that she told you she was not very happy, but did not appear especially sad or cast down ... in fact, neither her words nor her attitude showed any thought of attempted suicide. Am I not right?"

Marie Pascal hesitated; she seemed worried over something; at length she spoke up:

"I do know more."

"What?"

Juve, to cover the young girl's confusion, had turned his head away while putting the last question.

"Why," he remarked, "you can see Mlle. d'Orsel's apartment from your windows!"

"Yes, Monsieur, and that..."

"Were you in bed when the suicide took place?"

"No ...I was not in bed, I saw..."

"Ah! You saw! What did you see?"

"Monsieur, I haven't spoken to a soul about it; in fact, I'm not sure I wasn't mistaken, it all happened so quickly....I was getting a breath of fresh air at the window, I noticed her apartment was lighted up, I could see that through the curtains, and I said to myself, her lover must have arrived."

"Well, what then?"

"Then suddenly some one pulled back the hall-window curtains, then the window was flung open and I thought I saw a man holding Mlle. d'Orsel by the shoulders ...she was struggling but without crying out ...finally he threw her out of the window, then the light was extinguished and I saw nothing more."

"But you called for help?"

"Ah, Monsieur, I'm afraid I didn't act as I should have. I lost my head, you understand ...I left my room and was on my way downstairs to help the poor woman ...and then I heard voices, doors slamming ...I was afraid the murderer might kill me, too, so I hurried back to my room."

"According to you, then, it was not a suicide?"

"Oh, no, Monsieur ...I am quite sure she was thrown out of the window by some man."

"Some man? But, Mademoiselle, you know Susy d'Orsel was alone with the King, so that man must be the King."

Marie Pascal gave a dubious shrug.

"You know the King?" Juve asked.

"Yes, I sold him laces. I saw him through an open door."

"And you are not sure that he is or is not the murderer?"

"No, I don't know, that's why I've said nothing about it. I'm not sure of anything."

"Pardon, Mademoiselle, but it seems to me you don't quite grasp the situation ...what is it you are not sure of?"

"Whether it was the King who killed poor Mlle. Susy."

"But you are sure it was a man who killed Mlle. d'Orsel?"

"Yes, Monsieur ...and I am also sure it was a thin, tall man ...in fact, some one of the same build as the King."

"Well, Mademoiselle, I cannot see why you have kept this knowledge to yourself, it is most important, for it does away with the theory of suicide, it proves that a crime has been committed."

"Yes, but if it wasn't the King, it would be terrible to suspect him unjustly ...that is what stopped me..."

"It must no longer stop you. If the King is a murderer, he must be punished like any other man; if he is innocent, the guilty man must be caught. You haven't spoken of this to the concièrge?"

Marie Pascal smiled.

"No, Monsieur, Mme. Ceiron is rather a gossip."

"I understand, but now you need keep silence no longer; in fact, I should be glad if you would spread your news ...talk of it freely and I, on my side, will notify my chief....I may add that we shall not be long in clearing up this mystery."

Juve had a reason for giving this advice. The more gossip, the less chance would the police department have to stifle the investigation.

Marie Pascal slept badly that night. She was too intelligent not to realize that her deposition had convinced Juve of the guilt of the King, and this troubled her greatly. She, herself, was persuaded that she had seen the King throw Susy out of the window, although she had had no time to identify him positively and the young girl was alarmed at the importance of her testimony.

However, she determined to follow Juve's advice and spread the gossip. With that purpose she went down to see Mother Ceiron. As the concièrge was not in her room she called through the hallway:

"Madame Ceiron!...Madame Ceiron!"

A man's voice answered and a laundryman came downstairs carrying a basket.

"The concièrge is on the sixth floor, Mademoiselle. I passed her as I was going up to get M. de Sérac's laundry."

"Ah, thank you, then I will wait for her."

Marie Pascal took a seat in the office, but at the end of ten minutes she became bored and decided to go out and get a breath of the fresh morning air.

As she reached the entrance she noticed an article of clothing lying on the ground.

"A woman's chemise," she exclaimed, picking it up. "The laundryman must have dropped it."

Then suddenly she grew pale and retraced her steps to the office.

"Good God!" she cried, leaning for support upon the back of a chair.

CHAPTER VII
THE KING RECEIVES

The elegant attaché of the Secretary for Foreign Affairs bowed, saying:

"I am extremely sorry to bring your Majesty this bad news."

A voice from the depth of the cushions inquired:

"What bad news?"

"I am telling your Majesty that it would be difficult — even impossible for you to go to the Longchamps races as you had the intention of doing."

"And why not?"

"The President of the Republic opens to-day the exposition at the Bagatelle Museum. If your Majesty went to the Bois de Boulogne you would run the risk of meeting him. You would then be obliged to stop and talk a few moments, but as this interview has not been foreseen and arranged for it would be very awkward."

"That is true."

"That is all I had to convey to your Majesty."

"Let me see, what is your name, Monsieur?"

"I am Count Adhemar de Candières, your Majesty."

"Well, Count, many thanks! You may retire."

The Count gracefully bowed himself out and with a convulsive movement of the cushions Jerome Fandor sprang up and burst out laughing.

"Ah!" he cried, "I thought that chap would never go! Your Majesty!... Sire ... the King ... pleasant names to be called when you're not accustomed to them. I've already had twenty-four hours of it, and if it goes on much longer I shall begin to think it's not a joke.

"And the King himself, what's become of him ... what is Frederick-Christian II doing now ... that's something I'd like to find out."

The journalist had indeed sufficient food for thought. From the dawn of New Year's Day he had gone from surprise to surprise. At first he thought he had been brought to the Royal Palace Hotel at the instigation of the King. That would have been the simple solution of the affair. The King must have realized the awkward predicament in which his companion was placed and in spite of his drunken stupor he would come to his assistance as soon as possible. As a matter of fact, Fandor had been set at liberty. The journalist therefore had waited patiently for the arrival of the King, who was unaccountably late.

Then little by little it began to dawn on him that the hotel people were considering him not as a friend of the King but as the King himself! Under ordinary circumstances, he would at once have made his identity known, but against that there were now a multitude of objections. His presence in the apartment of the murdered Susy d'Orsel had created an ambiguous and disagreeable situation. Again, was the personnel of the hotel really duped by the substitution?

The situation was becoming more and more difficult for Fandor. He realized that he was being watched. The evening before one of the clerks of the Royal Palace Hotel had informed him that his Majesty's automobile was ready. For a moment Fandor did not know what to do, but finally decided to take a chance for an outing. As soon as he had come downstairs he regretted his decision. Among the persons lounging in the lobby he recognized five or six detectives whom he had known and he realized that the police would have accurate information as to where he might go. On reaching the door he saw three or four automobiles lined up outside. Which one belonged to the King? Faced by this situation he acted without hesitation, he turned quickly and went back to the Royal apartment, where during the rest of the evening he had been left in peace. The following morning he awoke with a violent headache, and applied the usual remedy for the neuralgia to which he was subject. He bound up his head with a large silk scarf which he found in the Royal wardrobe. During the course of the morning his hotel bill was brought to him, which amounted to four thousand francs.

"Pretty stiff," he muttered, "for three days' stay. It may be all right for Frederick-Christian II, but for a poor devil of a journalist it is rather awkward."

Fandor was wondering what he should do about it when the telephone rang to announce a visitor. After listening at the receiver, his face suddenly lighted with a broad smile.

"Show him up," he answered.

Several moments afterwards a man entered the apartment He was about forty and wore the conventional frock coat and light gloves.

"I am," he said, "the private secretary of the Comptoir National de Crédit and am at your Majesty's disposition for the settlement of accounts. Your Majesty will excuse our sub-director for not having come himself to take your orders as it is his pleasure and honor generally to do, but he has been ill for several days and that is why I have begged permission for this audience with your Majesty."

Fandor with difficulty repressed his desire to laugh and congratulated himself that he had escaped the danger of being shown up by the sub-director who knew the real King. The Secretary brought with him a large sum of money which he placed at the disposal of the sovereign. For a moment Fandor was tempted to accept the money but his scruples held him back. If things should turn out badly it would not do to lay himself open to the charge of usurping the Royal funds as well as the personality of the King. So he limited himself to handing over the hotel bill, saying:

"Kindly settle this without delay and don't stint yourself with the tips."

A little later a porter entered with newspapers. Fandor seized them eagerly, but after a single glance he could not repress a movement of impatience.

"These idiots," he growled to himself, "always bring me the Hesse-Weimar papers, and I don't know a confounded word of German. What I would like to get hold of is a copy of *La Capitale.*"

He rang the bell intending to give the order for a copy to be sent up, but at that moment a servant announced:

"Mlle. Marie Pascal is here, your Majesty."

"What does she want?"

The servant handed Fandor a letter.

"Your Majesty has granted an interview to her."

Without thinking the journalist asked: "Is she pretty?"

The employé of the Royal Palace kept a straight face. He was too much in the habit of dealing with royal patrons. The King might joke as much as he pleased, but the same liberty was not granted to others. He therefore made a deep bow and said with a tone of profound deference:

"I will send Marie Pascal to your Majesty."

CHAPTER VIII
MARIE PASCAL

Now that he had become a King and was obliged to receive unexpected visits in that capacity, Fandor had adopted the wise precaution of making his visitors wait in the main Salon, while he retired to the adjoining study. From there, thanks to a large mirror, he could see them without being seen himself. Following this precaution he waited for the appearance of his visitor and scarcely had she set foot in the Salon when he experienced an agreeable surprise.

"Ah, there's a pretty girl."

He was right. She was charming, with her large clear blue eyes, her fair hair and slight figure.

"By Jove," thought Fandor, "here's a way to fill up my hours of solitude. It oughtn't to be hard for one in my position to get up an intrigue, and provided the lady is not too shy I can begin one of those adventures one reads of in fairy stories."

Covering his face still further with his scarf and putting on a pair of blue spectacles he entered the Salon. The young girl betrayed a slight movement of surprise upon seeing him. At his silent invitation she sat down on the edge of an armchair without daring to raise her eyes. Then followed a long pause, until Fandor recollected that according to etiquette she was waiting for him to speak first.

"Well, Mademoiselle, what can I do for you?"

The young girl stammered: "I wanted to see you ... pardon ... to see your Majesty ... to tell him how grateful I am for the laces he ordered from me ... that your Majesty ordered."

Fandor began to be amused at the embarrassment of the young girl, so to set her at ease he remarked:

"Mademoiselle, just talk to me as you would to anyone else, and as for the laces, I shall be very glad to order others."

A start of surprise from Marie Pascal gave Fandor the uneasy feeling that he had made a break.

"Then, your Majesty, I suppose I must send the next lot to the Queen."

"Of course."

"How about the bill?"

Fandor repressed a smile. Evidently these poor Kings must have one hand in their pockets. As the interview continued the young girl regained her confidence, and going close to Fandor, spoke in a tone of sincere anxiety:

"Sire, it was not you ... oh, forgive me." And then in a lower tone: "I have denounced you, Sire."

Then, dropping to her knees, Marie Pascal repeated all that had happened. Fandor now realized that the death of Susy d'Orsel had a witness and that a detective was now in possession of the facts.

"And this detective! Is he tall, broad shouldered, about forty-five, with gray hair and clean shaven?"

The young girl was astonished at the accuracy of the portrait.

"Why, yes, Sire ... your Majesty is right."

"It can be no other than Juve," thought Fandor joyfully. Then turning to Marie Pascal, "Now you must answer truthfully the question I am going to ask you. Will you tell me why, after accusing me of this dreadful crime, you have suddenly changed your opinion and come to tell me how sorry you are and that you are now sure I am not guilty? You must have very serious reasons for this change of front."

"I have been convinced of your innocence," she replied, "by the most absolute proof." She then recounted to Fandor her discovery of the chemise belonging to the Marquis de Sérac.

"After picking up this chemise I was about to give it over to Mme. Ceiron, the concièrge of the house, when my eyes happened to fall upon the ruffles on the sleeves. Attached to the right sleeve were some shreds of lace which seemed to have been torn from a larger piece. I am a lace maker and I recognized immediately that these pieces came from a dress I had just delivered to Mlle. Susy d'Orsel a few hours before."

Fandor, who was listening with the closest attention, now asked: "What do you deduce from that, Mademoiselle?"

"Sire, simply that the person who threw Susy d'Orsel out of the window was wearing that chemise."

"And," continued the journalist, "as this belonged to the Marquis de Sérac?"

"But it is a woman's chemise."

Fandor quickly realized the importance of this testimony. First, that Susy d'Orsel had really been murdered and secondly that the King Frederick-Christian had had no hand in it.

"Is your Majesty very unhappy over the death of Mlle. d'Orsel?"

Fandor glanced sharply at the young woman and then replied enigmatically: "I am, of course, very much shocked at the tragic end of this poor girl. But what is the matter with you?"

Marie Pascal was growing paler and paler and finally collapsed in his arms. Gently he placed Marie Pascal on a sofa. For a few moments Fandor sat there holding her hands. Then she sat up quickly.

"What are you doing?"

Ready to continue what he considered an amusing adventure, he was about to take her in his arms murmuring, "I love you." But she rose quickly and fled horror-stricken.

"No, no, it's horrible." She sank down covering her face and crying hysterically.

Fandor rushed over just in time to hear her murmur, "Alas, and I love you."

A variety of sentiments and impressions passed through the mind of Fandor. At first, delighted with the avowal he had heard, he took her, unresisting, in his arms. Then suddenly he became the victim of a violent jealousy. For it was not to Fandor she had yielded but to the King of Hesse-Weimar, Frederick-Christian. She looked so pretty with her tears and her love that the situation became intolerable to him.

"Sire," whispered the gentle voice of Marie Pascal, "may I remind you of a promise? Dare I ask for a souvenir?" She pointed to a photograph of Frederick-Christian II.

"All right, all right," growled Fandor, "take it."

She then handed him a pen and asked him to write a dedication.

"No, I'll be hanged if I do," cried Fandor. Then seeing that the young girl was beginning to cry again, he added:

"My dear Marie Pascal, I am very sorry but it is against the rule for me to write a single word on my portrait....It is against the Constitution." The journalist searched through his pockets to find something he might give her as compensation, and then clasped her to his heart as the only thing possible to do under the circumstances. At this moment a servant entered and gravely announced:

"Sire, Wulfenmimenglaschk is here." Had the sun or the moon or the King himself been announced Fandor's amazement would not have been greater. Marie Pascal was about to slip away embarrassed, hardly capable of leaving in so much happiness, when Fandor recalled her.

"Mademoiselle!"

"Sire!"

"What you told me just now about the torn lace you had better repeat at police headquarters." Then in a lower tone he continued his instructions. When he had finished she nodded her head.

Yes, she would go and find Juve, the detective Juve, as the King had ordered her, and she would tell him everything.

The servant was waiting motionless for the King's answer.

"Wulfenmimenglaschk," thought he, "that must be one of those extraordinary German-American cocktails which Frederick-Christian is accustomed to order." He turned to the servant:

"Pour it out." At the man's surprise Fandor realized that he had made a mistake. At this moment a very fat man with scarlet face and pointed moustache appeared in the doorway and gave the military salute, announcing in a voice of thunder:

"Wulfenmimenglaschk!"

"Good God," murmured the journalist, dropping into an armchair. "This time I'm dished. He's come from Hesse-Weimar."

CHAPTER IX
A PARTY OF THREE

Juve was busy searching in a bureau drawer while Marie Pascal was going through piles of linen in her cupboard.

"You are sure you put it there?" asked Juve. "Madame Ceiron hasn't by any chance taken it away, has she?"

"Oh, no," replied Marie Pascal, "I am quite sure I locked it in my drawer, and locked the door of my room as well."

The room had been turned completely topsy-turvy, while Juve and Marie Pascal were searching anxiously and nervously through all the girl's belongings.

When she left the Royal Palace Hotel, Marie Pascal had gone directly to Police Headquarters, where she had found Juve. After telling him the history of the chemise fallen from the Marquis de Sérac's laundry, she had repeated all the details of her interview with the King and the advice he had given her.

"His Majesty Frederick-Christian was certainly wise in sending you here," he replied; "to begin with, it proves most conclusively that he has every intention of denying the crime of which you accused him yesterday, and of which you no longer accuse him to-day."

Marie Pascal protested: "I never accused him!"

"It amounted to the same thing, for the man you say threw Susy d'Orsel out of the window could only be the King, since he was alone with his mistress....Now we get the further evidence of the chemise found by you quite by chance ...and by sending you to His Majesty explicitly accuses a woman, the woman to whom that chemise belonged — of having killed Susy d'Orsel."

"The first thing to be done, Mademoiselle, is to go to your room and have a look at this garment. The Marquis de Sérac himself is away, and besides, his reputation is well known. Therefore, we cannot accuse him. If the chemise was found among his laundry it would imply that the murderer, taken by surprise, hid himself in the Marquis's apartment and either changed his clothes there or dropped the chemise into the Marquis's laundry-bag on purpose to create a false scent."

Without further words, Juve and the young girl drove to Rue de Monceau to examine the chemise which she had found that morning. Marie Pascal unlocked her door; a few moments later started in amazement. The chemise had disappeared. Afterward Juve began to wonder whether Marie Pascal had spoken the truth or whether it was a put-up story between herself and the King.

"There's no use looking any further," he cried, "some one has stolen it."

"But it's terrible," replied Marie Pascal. "It is the only evidence that would clear the King. The only proof that he is not guilty. How can anyone be sure that I really found the chemise?"

Juve nodded. "That's what I have been asking myself, Mademoiselle."

"Oh, what can be done?"

The anxiety of the young girl interested Juve keenly.

"It's very annoying, Mademoiselle. But, after all, it only affects you indirectly. The King will have to explain clearly whether he was alone with Susy d'Orsel or whether a woman accompanied him."

"Yes, but then they will suspect him....Oh, M. Juve, what do you think?"

Juve gave a dry cough and answered:

"Well, Mademoiselle, this is the way I figure it out. Susy d'Orsel has been the mistress of the King for about two years, and as you know constancy is unusual with men, it is quite possible that Frederick-Christian had had enough of his mistress and had become interested in another woman."

"That doesn't explain anything."

"Oh, yes, it does. It explains everything. Suppose, for instance, that the King had fallen in love with another demi-mondaine, and that had brought her to the apartment to notify Susy d'Orsel of his intention to break with her. Might not a quarrel have arisen between the two women and the new mistress, exasperated by some taunt, had thrown the unfortunate Susy d'Orsel out of the window?...That would be a commonplace enough story."

While speaking Juve was watching carefully the expression on Marie Pascal's face. She had grown very pale and at the end protested with a cry:

"No, no, you are wrong. The King had not two mistresses. And besides, the chemise I found was made of coarse linen, and would not certainly be worn by that sort of woman."

"Ah," thought Juve, "I wonder if Marie Pascal by any chance is in love with his Majesty. That would explain many things. To begin with, the reason why she was watching Susy's window. Also why the King, touched perhaps by the caprice of this girl, had had a row with his mistress, and finally why Marie Pascal, having seen him again, had invented the story of the chemise, which could not be found. This young girl is imprudent. She lets it be seen too clearly how disagreeable the hypothesis would be to her. After reasoning thus to himself Juve turned to the young girl.

"Well, Mademoiselle Marie, if my supposition is wrong there can be only one explanation, namely, that some woman committed the crime, a woman who was hidden in the apartment and who subsequently hid the chemise in the Marquis de Sérac's laundry bag, and then having learned of your discovery returned to your room to recover the compromising article." Marie Pascal remained silent. Juve continued with the intention of alarming her out of her reserve.

"But if this last supposition is the right one we must admit that it is none the less unfortunate for the King. For once the chemise disappeared the King must be held guilty until further discovery."

Marie Pascal replied simply:

"It is frightful. The more so because I had this proof in my hand, and I know very well he is innocent."

Juve picked up his hat and began buttoning his overcoat.

"Naturally, Mademoiselle, you yourself know ...and I may add that I am of your opinion, but still you have no proof to offer, and consequently...."

Marie Pascal wrung her hands in desperation.

"What is to be done? How can the truth come to light....Ah, I shall never forgive myself for having at first accused the King and then losing the proof of his innocence."

"Oh, don't take it to heart too much. In criminal affairs the first results of the investigator are really conclusive."

Juve nodded to the young girl and rapidly went downstairs smiling to himself. One thing and one alone had developed from his interview. The King denied his guilt.

"The only thing I know," he thought, "is that the concièrge affirms that Frederick-Christian was alone when he came to see Susy d'Orsel....If I can prove that definitely I can also prove by the chain of evidence that the King is guilty. But how to do it?"

Juve hurried through the courtyard, passing the office of Mme. Ceiron, who was out at that moment. As he had already obtained the key of Susy d'Orsel's apartment, her absence did not trouble him.

"I'll be willing to bet," he thought, "that I shall find nothing interesting in her rooms. But it is at least my duty to go over them carefully....If only I could discover evidence showing that three persons were there together, but that is most unlikely. The officers, the doctors, the concièrge and the men who carried the body to the Morgue would have destroyed all traces."

It was not without a slight shudder that Juve entered the apartment where the tragedy occurred. With a real catch at his heart he went through the bright, luxuriously decorated rooms, still giving evidence of a feminine presence.

Death had entered there. The sinister death of crime, brutal, unforeseen. A hundred times more tragic for remaining unexplained. Juve, however, quickly stifled his feelings. He was there to investigate and nothing else mattered. The bedroom presented nothing worthy of notice, the boudoir was in perfect order, also the kitchen and the hall.

Juve entered, finally, the dining-room. It was there, according to the testimony of witnesses, that the crime must have taken place. It was there in any case that Susy d'Orsel had received her lover.

Nothing had been deranged. The table was still set for supper. Two places, side by side, bore mute witness that the King had been alone with his mistress.

Juve at first carefully examined the general lay of the room. The disposition of the chairs, the two knives from the two forks, two fish plates, all went to prove there had been only two persons at the table.

But suddenly he gave a start and his face expressed the keenest interest. He dropped to his knees and carefully examined the floor under the table.

"Unless I am dreaming there are ashes here."

Juve bent forward and noticed at the right of the sofa an ash receiver placed near the edge of the table, and below on the carpet a small heap of gray ash.

"To begin with, we'll admit that Susy d'Orsel flicked the ash off her cigarette ... gray ash from Egyptian tobacco, a woman's cigarette."

He now moved to the left of the sofa.

"In the second place, here is another heap of ashes in this plate ... cigar ashes ... in fact here is the tend showing a German brand.... So the King was sitting on the right of Susy d'Orsel. Less careful, he used his plate instead of an ash receiver."

Now bending down he noticed on the carpet a third heap of ash.

"A third person has been smoking here. For there is no reason why the King should have changed his place and sat at the opposite side of the table where no place is laid.... Also this third person, in smoking a cigarette, and having no plate or ash receiver, dropped his ashes on the carpet."

After a moment's thought Juve took from his pocket a small automatic lighting arrangement and going on his hands and knees under the table began a careful examination of its feet. In a moment he gave an exclamation of joy.

"Ah, I have got it now. This is conclusive."

And in fact Juve had made a most important discovery. The heavy legs of the table were joined by crosspieces and Juve had been able to determine where Susy d'Orsel had rested her feet. He saw also the slight traces of mud where the King had rested his feet. Most important, however, was the fact that further traces of mud had been left by a third pair of feet.

"If only I could identify the feet that were placed here, and whether they belonged to a woman."

A closer examination of the wood made him rise to his feet with a cry. Quickly taking a chair, he placed it before the table in the place that might naturally be occupied by a third guest, and then sat down. This is what he discovered. It was quite impossible for a woman to have been sitting there. Having stretched his legs and rested his feet upon the traces of mud, he discovered that one of the legs of the table came directly between his knees. A woman's skirt would have made this position impossible for her.

"Why, the King was telling the truth! There were three persons in this dining-room a few moments before the crime was committed. And they were Susy d'Orsel, the King and another man."

Juve now threw himself into an armchair and remained buried in thought.

"To sum it up, the King alone is in a position to give me further information.... And if he should refuse to speak or should attempt to lie I have now within my hands the means of forcing him to tell the truth."

He sprang up quickly.

"The next thing to do is to go and see the King."

CHAPTER X
WULFENMIMENGLASCHK

Wulfenmimenglaschk!

Fandor stared in consternation at the individual who had just entered the apartment of Frederick-Christian II.

He was enormously fat and absurd looking. A large red nose stood out between two little blinking eyes; a heavy moustache bushed above his three well-defined chins. In his hand he held a soft green hat, through the ribbon of which was stuck a feather. He wore a wide leather belt containing cartridge cases, and the butts of two revolvers peeped out of his pockets.

The man began once more.

"Wulfen..."

Fandor stopped him with a movement of impatience.

"Won't you please speak French, so long as we are in France?"

For the twenty-fifth time this strange individual repeated the phrase which apparently meant his name and added in French:

"Head of the Secret Service of the Kingdom of Hesse-Weimar and Attaché of your Majesty."

Fandor congratulated himself that the table separated them. He expected at any moment to be shown up as an impostor. But thinking the best plan would be to try and bluff it through he said graciously:

"Sit down, Monsieur Wulf."

"But that isn't possible."

"Yes, it is ... take that chair."

"I should never dare to," answered the police officer.

Fandor insisted.

"We desire you."

Wulf bowed to such formal instructions, murmuring:

"I do so at the order of your Majesty."

Fandor sprang up amazed.

"Does he take me for the King too? That can't be possible. The head of the Secret Service! They must be carrying this joke out to the bitter end. I'm hanged if I can understand it."

"What do you want?"

The man who since his entrance had not taken his eyes off Fandor, now appeared to be considering him with the greatest admiration.

"Ah! Heaven be thanked....My most cherished desire has come to pass....Your Majesty has been good enough to allow me the honor of a personal interview."

"He must be mad," thought Fandor.

"Of course I was well acquainted with your august features....Frederick-Christian II is popular in his kingdom ...his portrait hangs on the walls of private houses as well as public buildings. But your Majesty understands that portraits and the reality are often dissimilar....Now, although for seventeen years I have belonged to the Secret Service of the Kingdom, I have never before had the honor of meeting his Majesty face to face."

"So, Monsieur Wulf, you think I don't look like my portrait."

"Pardon me, Sire, that is not what I wish to say. The portrait represents your Majesty as being taller and heavier, with a larger moustache and fairer hair."

"In other words," said Fandor, smiling, "my portrait flatters me."

"Oh, Sire, quite the contrary, I assure you."

"Well, what do you want?"

Wulf was evidently waiting for this question. He rose from the seat and made a careful inspection of the room, opening each door to see that no one was outside listening. Then he returned to Fandor and whispered:

"I am here on a secret mission, Sire."

"Well, let's hear what it is."

"I am charged with two commissions, one which interests your Majesty, the other the Kingdom. To begin with, I have come to get your reply to the telegram in cipher which his Highness the Minister of the Interior sent your Majesty yesterday."

"The deuce," thought Fandor, "this is getting annoying. What on earth shall I tell him?"

Then with an air of innocence he asked:

"What telegram are you speaking of? I have received none."

"Your Majesty didn't receive it?"

"Well, you know the service is rotten in France."

"Yes," replied Wulf scornfully, "it's easy to see it's a Republic."

Fandor smiled. If he was compelled to run down his own country for once, it wouldn't matter.

"What can you expect with the continual strikes ... however, that's not our fault, is it, Wulf?"

"Quite true, Sire."

The Chief of the Secret Service leaned toward Fandor and whispered mysteriously.

"I have it, Sire."

"What," inquired Fandor, with somewhat of anxiety.

"The text of the telegram."

Wulf drew out a document and was about to hand it to Fandor, but the latter stopped him with a gesture.

"Read it to me."

"His Highness, the Minister of the Interior, begs to inform your Majesty that since his absence a propaganda unfavorable to the throne is being actively spread in the Court and in the town. The partisans of Prince Gudulfin believe the occasion favorable to seize the Government."

Fandor pretended anger.

"Ah, it's Prince Gudulfin again!"

"Alas, Sire, it is always the Prince."

Fandor repressed a violent laugh.

"Is that all?"

"No, Sire. His Highness the Minister requested to know, in the name of the Queen, when your Majesty has the intention of returning to his Kingdom."

Fandor rose and tapping Wulf amicably on the shoulder replied:

"Tell the Queen that business of the greatest importance keeps me in Paris, but that before long I hope to return to the Court."

Wulf looked at him without answering, and Fandor added with great dignity:

"You can go now."

"But I have a formal order not to return to Glotzbourg without your Majesty, and when your Majesty is ready I am at your orders. Even to-night."

Then he added in a low tone:

"That would be a pity, for in Paris..."

Fandor glanced quickly at him. So this fat police officer was like the rest of the world. He, too, wanted to have his fling in Paris.

At this moment they were interrupted by the arrival of the servant carrying a tray of cocktails. Fandor turned smilingly to Wulf.

"Have a cocktail, Wulf?"

The officer almost choked with delight. In Hesse-Weimar he would never have imagined that his King could be so charming and simple in private life. He made some remark to this effect and the journalist answered:

"Why not, Wulf? Hesse-Weimar and France are two different places ... we are now in a democracy, let's be democratic." Then clinking his glass with Wulf's he cried:

"To the health of the Republic!"

Fandor now led the conversation to the charms and seductions of Paris, and he pictured the delights of the city in such glowing terms that Wulf's little eyes sparkled and his purple face became even more congested. He lost his timidity. He expressed a wish to see the Moulin-Rouge and the Singing Fountains.

"What do you know about them?" inquired Fandor.

"Why, they speak of nothing else in Hesse-Weimar."

"You shall hear them then....Look here, Wulf, are you married?"

"Yes, Sire."

"Then I'll bet you deceive your wife."

"Hum! I should be sorry if my wife heard you say that. For up to now..."

Fandor laughed.

"Oh, we Kings know everything. Even more than your Secret Service."

"That's true," cried Wulf, "absolutely true."

"Wulf, Paris is the town of charming women. I am sure they will please you greatly. And as I have no need of your services to-morrow I will give you your liberty."

The officer was about to break into thanks when the door opened and a servant announced:

"Will your Majesty receive Monsieur Juve?"

"Show him in."

When the detective entered and heard Fandor addressed as His Majesty he opened his eyes and stood staring, while Fandor himself was obliged to stuff his handkerchief into his mouth to prevent himself from roaring with laughter.

Juve began:

"What does this mean?..."

But Fandor quickly stepped forward.

"Monsieur Juve, let me introduce you to Monsieur Wulf. Monsieur Wulf is the head of the Secret Service in my Kingdom of Hesse-Weimar."

Then tapping Wulf familiarly on the shoulder he added:

"He's one of the greatest detectives in the world. He was able to find the King of Hesse-Weimar right here in this apartment....Though he had never seen me, he found me and recognized me!"

The officer beamed with delight at the compliment. Fandor then conducted him to the door, whispering advice as to the best way of passing his night in Paris.

Scarcely had the ridiculous Wulf disappeared when Juve seized Fandor by the shoulder.

"Fandor! What does this mean?"

"Why, Juve, simply that I'm the King of Hesse-Weimar — of which fact you had a proof just now."

But Juve's face was serious.

"Now, without joking, tell me what you are doing here."

When Fandor had finished his explanation Juve seized him by the hand.

"Where is the King, Fandor?"

"I have already told you. I haven't the least idea. And, furthermore, I don't care."

"You are crazy to talk this way. What is happening is extremely serious."

"Why?"

"Simply because a charge of murder has been brought against Frederick-Christian."

"Very few people know it," exclaimed the journalist.

He stopped speaking suddenly. Outside the murmur of a crowd grew louder and louder as it approached. Juve and Fandor ran to the window just in time to receive a volley of stones which broke the glass in several places. The two men sprang back.

"Put out the lights!" cried Juve.

Below them the avenue was black with people. After a moment they could distinguish what they were shouting.

"Murderer! Murderer! Down with the King!"

"That surprises you, Fandor," exclaimed Juve, "but for the last forty-eight hours I have been watching this trouble grow, and I tell you it is going to end badly."

At the head of the mob and more daring than the others appeared a strange individual. A long-bearded old man, dressed in white, was endeavoring to force his way into the hotel and a fight was taking place at the door.

"I know him," muttered Juve, "I have seen him once or twice before trying to raise a row about this affair."

"Why it's Ouaouaoua, the Primitive Man," cried Fandor.

A squad of policemen now arrived on the scene, and without much difficulty succeeded in dispersing the mob.

"Well, Juve."

"Well, Fandor."

"To tell you the truth, Juve," admitted the journalist, "I am beginning to get a little uneasy. However, this manifestation is against Frederick-Christian, not against me...."

Juve interrupted.

"Idiot, don't you understand what's happening? Either one of two things. You are the King, and therefore in the opinion of the public the murderer of Susy d'Orsel, or you are not the King, and in that case you are an impostor, which will make it all the more likely that you will be considered as the murderer."

"Not much," cried Fandor. "You seem to forget it was I who picked up..."

"Who knows that?" continued Juve. "Why, my dear fellow, think for a moment, if the King is guilty, and even if he is not, he will be only too glad to throw the responsibility for this tragedy upon your shoulders.... That would let him out of it completely. The situation could not be much worse. Suppose that this evening, to-morrow, at any moment some one finds out that you are not the King, you will then not only be suspected of the murder of Susy d'Orsel, but you will be accused of having done away with the King.... Where is the King? You haven't the least idea. Then what answer could you make?"

"The devil," murmured Fandor, suddenly growing pale. "I didn't think of that. You are right, Juve, I am in a bad fix."

There was a moment of silence. The two men looked at one another, troubled and anxious. Then Fandor, struck by a sudden inspiration, seized his hat and cane.

"What are you doing?" inquired Juve.

"I ... Why I'm going to clear out."

"How?... The King's apartment is surrounded by Secret Service men.... They take good care of His Majesty.... You were forgetting that!"

"That's true," said Fandor, depressed. "So now I am actually a prisoner. Look here, Juve, what has become of this Frederick-Christian? Haven't you any clue to follow?"

"No."

"He can't have vanished into thin air. We must find him if it is humanly possible."

"That's my opinion, Fandor, but I am wondering how."

And then suddenly to each of them the same thought occurred.

Fantômas!

Was it not probable that the strange crime of which Susy d'Orsel was the victim, the mysterious disappearance of the King, might be attributed to this enigmatic and redoubtable bandit?

It would not have been the first time that the journalist and the detective had put forth a similar hypothesis.

Fantômas had always symbolized the very essence of crime itself.

CHAPTER XI
ONE HUNDRED AND TWENTY-SEVEN STATIONS

On leaving Fandor, Juve walked up the Avenue Champs Elysées, refusing the offers of various cab drivers. He felt the need of movement as an antidote to his growing worry over the affair. On arriving at the Rue Saussaies, Juve sent up his card to M. Annion and requested an immediate interview. In a few moments he was shown into M. Annion's office.

"Well, what's new? What's the result of your investigation, Juve?"

"There is nothing much to report yet. The theory of suicide is possible, although a crime may have been committed. Whether the King is involved or not in this affair is still uncertain. It will take me a week at least to find out."

"In other words, you know nothing yet. Well, I can tell you a few things you don't know. Pass me those documents."

M. Annion looked through the papers and then continued:

"When Vicart saw you this morning he forgot to give you some of the instructions I had charged him with....I sent two of my men to the Royal Palace Hotel....Do you know what they found?"

"No, I haven't the least idea. There was nothing to learn at the Royal Palace itself."

"On the contrary, they made an extraordinary discovery."

"What was it?"

"They discovered that the King is not the King. The individual who is posing as Frederick-Christian II is an impostor. Rather sensational news, isn't it?"

"So sensational that I don't believe it."

"And why not, if you please?"

Juve avoided a direct reply. He asked:

"Upon what do you place this supposed imposture?"

M. Annion took up the papers before him.

"I have the evidence here before me. But first I must tell you how our suspicions became aroused....This morning, after your departure, we received a telegram from Hesse-Weimar inquiring why Frederick-Christian did not reply to the telegram sent him from his kingdom.... That gave me an inkling of what was going on....I sent to the Royal Palace Hotel and there my two detectives learned that Frederick-Christian had gained the reputation of being extremely odd, in fact, half crazy. Furthermore, that he was acting in a manner totally different from that of former occasions. He now scarcely moves from his room, whereas previously he spent most of his time out of doors."

M. Annion handed Juve the documents and begged him to look them over himself. After returning them Juve realized that his best chance would be to gain time.

"This is going to cause a great deal of trouble. If an impostor is really installed in the Royal Palace Hotel we shall have to notify the Chancellor and ask for the authorization to verify ...In other words, a number of tiresome formalities will have to be complied with."

"Wait a minute, I have more surprises for you. We now have the press on our trail. All the evening papers publish articles inferring the guilt of the King....They come out boldly accusing him of murder. Would you believe that at seven o'clock this evening there was a shouting, howling mob in front of the Royal Palace? And so, my dear Juve, you had better take two men with you, and without delay go to the hotel and arrest the man who is passing for the King, and who is, besides, the murderer of Susy d'Orsel."

This is what Juve feared; he determined to make every effort to prevent the arrest of Fandor.

"All this is very well, but I think you will agree with me that it is a romance, Monsieur Annion."

"May I ask why you think that?"

"Certainly, Monsieur Annion.

"You intend to arrest the false King because he is accused by the public of murder....If he were the real King, would you be willing to arrest him without further proof?"

"No ... naturally not ... but then he is an impostor, so that won't worry me."

"Very good, Monsieur Annion, and now, suppose you have guessed wrong? After all, you are basing your conclusion upon a number of minor details, upon the observation of hotel clerks. All that is not sufficient. But don't you think anyone in Paris knows the King by sight?"

"Only two persons knew him here.... The Ambassador of Hesse-Weimar, M. de Naarboveck, who has just been changed and whose successor has not as yet arrived. The other person is one of his friends, the Marquis de Sérac, who happens to be away from Paris just now."

Juve smiled.

"You forget one man, Monsieur Annion, who knows the King better than either of these. I refer to the head of the Secret Service of Hesse-Weimar ... one of my colleagues. He is at present staying at the Royal Palace and sees the King every day. Consequently it will be scarcely possible to deceive him."

"What is his name?" asked M. Annion.

"It's rather complicated; he calls himself Wulfenmimenglaschk, which we may cut to Wulf for all practical purposes. What should you think of his testimony?"

M. Annion hesitated.

"Of course, if this individual knows the King..."

"He is attached to the King's person."

"And you are sure he recognized him at the Royal Palace?"

"I'll bring him here and let him speak for himself."

"Well, I'll give you until eleven to-morrow morning to produce this Wulf ... or whatever he calls himself; if then he cannot positively affirm that the King is really the King, you must arrest the impostor immediately. If, on the other hand, he does recognize him, we must refer the matter to the Minister of Foreign Affairs."

"That is understood," replied Juve, and he took his leave.

As Juve found himself again in the Rue de Saussaies his face clouded over.

"Twenty-four hours gained anyway, but I wonder where the devil I can get hold of this Wulf? I might catch him at the Moulin-Rouge ... Fandor sent him there."

Juve drove to the music hall and, showing his card, questioned the officials.

"I'm looking for a fat little man, probably slightly drunk, foreign accent, wears a brown coat, tight trousers, white spats, and is plastered all over with decorations."

"I saw him," cried one of the ushers. "I checked his overcoat and noticed the decorations. He left some time ago."

"Confound it!" muttered Juve. "You don't know why he left so early? The show is only beginning."

The usher smiled.

"Well, he carried a couple of girls away with him. Probably he's in some nearby café."

Juve decided to spend the whole night, if necessary, to find Wulf, and began a systematic search through all the cafés of Montmartre.

At length, about three in the morning, he decided to give himself a rest and take a drink. For this purpose he entered a small café at the corner of the Rue de Douai and the Rue Victor-Masse, and ordered a beer. He put the usual question:

"You don't happen to have seen a fat little man, drunk and profusely decorated?"

The proprietor at once grew excited.

"I should think I have seen him. He came in here asking for some outlandish brand of cigarettes, and ended by taking the cheapest I had, then paid for them with foreign money. And when I refused to take it, he threatened me with some King or other! Aren't we still a republic, I should like to know?"

Evidently, from the description, it could be no other than the peripatetic Wulf.

"Was he alone?" asked Juve.

"Oh, he brought in a little blonde with him, but when she saw his fake money, I guess she gave him the slip, for he turned to the right and she went up the street in the opposite direction."

"The devil!" exclaimed Juve; "the trail is lost again."

A waiter stepped forward.

"I think he went to the Courcelles Station; he asked me where it was."

"The Courcelles Station!"

Juve stood staring in amazement. What on earth could Wulf want to go there for?

"Have you a telephone?" he asked.

"Yes, Monsieur."

With great difficulty Juve succeeded in getting the connection.

"Hullo! Is that your Majesty?"

Fandor's voice replied, laughingly:

"Yes, it's His Majesty all right, but His Majesty doesn't like being wakened up at night. What can I do for you, my dear Juve?"

"Can you tell me where Wulf is?"

"How should I know? Probably with some women, he seems crazy about them."

"No, he hasn't any French money."

"Hold on, Juve; I advised him to take the circular tube as the best method of seeing Paris. I told him to stay on board till he reached the end of the line. Just a little joke of mine."

Fandor burst out laughing, and Juve rang off, angrily.

Once in the street, he stood a moment in doubt as to his next course. If Wulf was really taking a trip in the circular tube, he would be in process of going round and round Paris. How was it possible to overtake him?

Hailing a taxi, he explained to the chauffeur:

"Look here, I want you to take me to the Courcelles Station ... there we must find out in what direction the first train passes, either toward Porte Maillot or toward the Avenue de Clichy..."

The man stared stupidly and Juve found it necessary to explain in a few words the quest he was setting out upon.

"If our man isn't on the first train that passes Courcelles, then we must hurry over to the Bois de Boulogne Station, understand?"

Juve had the luck to learn from the ticket seller at Courcelles that she had noticed Wulf, and that he had bought a first-class ticket; this limited the search very considerably.

The first train pulled in, but Wulf was not on board.

Juve sprang into his taxi and now hurried over to the Bois de Boulogne. Here the same result met him; the next station was Auteuil, then Vaugirard, la Glacière and Bel-Air.

It was now eight o'clock, and his appointment with M. Annion was at eleven. What was to be done?

On reaching Menilmontant Station, Juve had about decided to abandon the chase.

"I'll wait for one more train and then make some other plan," he muttered.

By great good luck he caught sight of Wulf as it ran into the station. Rushing into the carriage, he seized his man and hauled him on to the platform.

"What's the matter? Why are you here, Monsieur Juve? I am perfectly amazed..."

"Where are you going, Monsieur Wulf?"

Wulf smiled fatuously:

"I have been following his Majesty's advice, seeing Paris. What an immense city! I counted one hundred and twenty-seven stations since five o'clock this morning and I have crossed ten rivers! Why have you stopped me? I wanted to go to the end of the line."

Juve bustled him into the waiting taxi.

"I'll explain as we go," he replied. "It is a question of saving the King. He is menaced by powerful and terrible enemies."

"I am ready to die for him," exclaimed Wulf. "What must I do?"

"Oh, it's not necessary to die. All you have to do is to certify before the police authorities that the person you know as Frederick-Christian at the Royal Palace is actually the King."

"I don't understand in the least what you mean!"

"That doesn't matter; you have only to do as I say and all will be well."

M. Annion was overcome.

Wulf, after testifying to the identity of the King, had been sent to wait in an adjoining room while Juve and M. Annion had a confidential chat.

"Well, Juve, I can't get over it. Without you, I should have made a terrible break! The King arrested! What a scandal! But, tell me, what's to be done now? The public's calling for the murderer. I place myself in your hands. What do you suggest?"

Juve thought a moment.

For the time being Fandor was safe, but he was still very far from being out of the woods.

"Monsieur Annion," he replied at length, "there is just one method of procedure in this case. The assassination of Susy d'Orsel, the question of this imposture, in fact all these mysterious points which have arisen cannot be cleared up in Paris."

"What the devil do you mean, Juve?"

"I mean that in all probability the threads of this intrigue lead to Hesse-Weimar, to the capital of the kingdom, to Glotzbourg. And, if you have no objection, I will start for there this evening."

"Go, go," replied M. Annion; "perhaps you are right ... anyhow, don't forget to take letters of introduction with you."

"Oh, don't worry about that. I can get all I want from my colleague."

"Your colleague?"

"Yes, from this excellent Wulf."

CHAPTER XII
CAMOUFLAGE

"Come in and sit down, Monsieur Wulfenmimenglaschk."

The Marquis de Sérac led the way into his study.

He was a powerfully built, white-haired man, in the sixties, still active, with a slightly tired voice, a typical man of the world in his manners and dress.

Very embarrassed, Wulf bowed and bowed:

"I am confused, Monsieur. Quite confused ... I ..."

"Not at all, Monsieur Wulf; now take off your overcoat, sit down and smoke a cigar. I assure you it's a great pleasure for me to talk to anyone coming from Hesse-Weimar. I left the court when I was very young, and I should be a stranger in Glotzbourg to-day; still I remember my very good friends there ... but never mind that now, we have more important subjects to discuss, Monsieur Wulf, and I'm sure you are in a hurry."

"Oh, not at all; I am only too happy and too proud ..."

"Yes, yes, Paris is a city of temptations, and I won't take too much of your time. First of all let me explain that I only received your letter yesterday, as I happened to be out of town. You state that I am in a position to render you a great service; this I shall be delighted to do as soon as you tell me what it is."

Wulf began a long and rambling story to the effect that upon leaving Glotzbourg for Paris, on his special mission to the King, he had conceived the idea of writing to the Marquis de Sérac, whom he knew to be an intimate friend of the King, to give him a letter of introduction to His Majesty.

"But now I don't need it," he ended, "for the King is my best friend ... he received me with charming simplicity, just like an old comrade."

"Alas, my dear Wulf, His Majesty is at present exposed to the most terrible danger."

"What do you mean?"

"You have doubtless heard of the tragic death of Mlle. Susy d'Orsel, the King's mistress, which, by a curious coincidence, occurred in this very house?"

"I know! I know!"

"Well, perhaps you also know that among the King's enemies, some dare to accuse him of having killed Mlle. Susy d'Orsel?"

"Oh! Such people ought to be cut in pieces."

"Alas, Monsieur Wulf, we are not yet in a position to avenge His Majesty. You don't happen to know who the real murderer is, do you?"

"No, I haven't the least idea; but if I ever get hold of him, I shall know what to do!"

The Marquis smiled and shrugged his shoulders:

"I shall be glad to help you."

"Thanks, Monsieur le Marquis, but I'm afraid we shan't succeed. There's a French detective on the case, a man named Juve, who hasn't been able to find the man either!"

The Marquis gave a slight start:

"Ah, and Juve has found nothing, suspects nobody?"

"No."

"That is strange.... Well, Monsieur Wulf, I think we shall be able to do better. You are ready for anything?"

"For everything, on my honor!" replied Wulf, with fervor.

"Very well, then I promise you we shall have some news within a week. But excuse me a moment, I have some orders to give; I won't be a moment."

The Marquis crossed the room and opened the door; Wulf could hear him talking:

"Is that you, Madame Ceiron?"

A woman's voice answered:

"Yes, Monsieur le Marquis. What can I do for you?"

"Kindly unpack the bag in my room and when you go out be sure to lock the doors. I don't want a recurrence of what happened the other day when some one entered my apartment and left a chemise belonging to the murderer among my laundry."

"Monsieur le Marquis may rest assured his orders will be obeyed."

In a few moments the Marquis returned and M. Wulf rose to go. He repeated with emphasis his determination:

"If ever I get the chance to arrest this murderer, I will do so in the face of any danger. All for the King! That is my motto!"

"Yes, you are right, Monsieur, all for the King."

The Marquis de Sérac bowed his visitor out, and then suddenly his smiling face underwent an astounding change of expression.

"I must clinch my alibi!"

In a moment he had torn off his false whiskers and his wig of white hair was quickly replaced by another — this time a woman's wig. With the agility of a Fregoli he then got into a skirt and waist.

Forty seconds after the departure of Wulf the Marquis de Sérac had become ...Madame Ceiron, the concièrge.

Three or four pencil marks and his disguise was complete. It would be impossible for anybody not having seen this transformation to guess that the Marquis de Sérac and old Madame Ceiron were one and the same individual.

After a quick glance into his mirror he rushed across his drawing-room, through the hall, and quickly opened a large Breton wardrobe. Through the centre of this rose a post which he seized and slid down. It was the same contrivance used by firemen to join their engines when a call was sent in. At the foot of the post in Madame Ceiron's apartment were stretched two mattresses to deaden the fall. These were placed in a small storeroom, well hidden from observation. After closing the door behind her, Madame Ceiron rushed to the hall in time to intercept Wulf on his way downstairs.

"You are looking for some one?" she asked.

"No, Madame, I have just come from the Marquis de Sérac's apartment."

After Wulf had disappeared Madame Ceiron returned to her office and was about to enter when a voice called:

"Here I am, Madame Ceiron. I found your note under my door. Is there anything I can do for you?"

"Ah, it's you, my child. You are very kind to have come, and there is something that you can do for me. I want to know if you will come upstairs to Susy d'Orsel's room with me."

"What on earth for?"

"Well, I'll tell you. It's this way: I am scared to go up there all alone."

Marie Pascal smiled.

"Of course it is rather appalling, but why do you go there, Madame Ceiron?"

"Well, you see, the police have put their seals over everything and I am paid one franc a day to see that nobody enters the apartment and breaks them. I have to take a look around from time to time, so won't you come with me?"

"Certainly, Madame Ceiron."

Marie Pascal and the concièrge went up together and began a careful examination of the poor girl's rooms. While the young girl was looking curiously around Madame Ceiron entered the boudoir. She crossed to the chimney and pulled out a small casket, which was hidden behind a blue curtain. She opened it quickly and inspected the contents.

"Jewels! Which would be the best to take? Ah, this ring and this bracelet ...and these earrings. Now for the key. I'll take that with me."

"Mam'zelle Marie Pascal!"

"Madame Ceiron?"

"Come along, my dear. I am so frightened, it upsets me to go through this poor girl's apartment. Just run and see if the outer door is locked."

While Marie Pascal turned her back and walked toward the door, Madame Ceiron suddenly pressed against a large box which fell over and spread a fine coal dust over the carpet.

"It is locked, Madame Ceiron."

"Then come along. I hope to Heaven this business will soon be cleared up or it will make me ill."

A few moments later Marie Pascal had returned to her own bedroom and the concièrge busied herself by opening in her office a parcel which she had taken from a cupboard. She was interrupted in her work by the arrival of a working woman who was engaged to take Madame Ceiron's place when she had errands to do.

"I am going to leave you alone here to-day, Madame. I have some shopping to do....I am going to spend my New Year's gifts, buy a green dress and a hat with red feathers....It is my turn to dress up a little."

Shortly afterwards the concièrge went out, taking with her the parcel she had prepared. But instead of going to the shopping district of Paris, she hurried toward the Bois de Boulogne.

When she had reached a remote part of the wood she entered a small hut. A few moments later visitors to the Bois noticed the well-known Ouaouaoua, the Primitive Man, walking down the main pathway. The enigmatic and dreamy face of this man resembled neither the Marquis de Sérac nor Madame Ceiron and yet...

The science of camouflage pushed to its extreme limits produces the most unexpected transformations.

CHAPTER XIII
THE KINGDOM OF HESSE-WEIMAR

"Has Monsieur le Baron any trunks to be examined? This is the Hesse-Weimar Customs."

These words, spoken in a respectful but guttural voice, startled Juve from the deep sleep into which he had fallen after a very unpleasant night. The detective opened his eyes and stretched himself.

The pale light of dawn struggled through the windows of the sleeping car, the curtains of which had been carefully drawn. Outside nothing was to be seen, for besides the mud which covered the windows a heavy fog lay over the country.

The train came to a standstill, and before Juve stood an individual dressed in an elegant blue and yellow uniform plentifully covered with gold braid. Juve looked around to see the man who was being addressed by the title of Monsieur le Baron and finally came to the conclusion that it was himself to whom the man was speaking.

"Why do you call me Monsieur le Baron?" The man touched his hat deferentially and seemed very surprised at the question.

"Why, Monsieur ... it's the custom. No one but the nobility travel first class."

Juve smiled and replied:

"That's all right, my friend, but in the future call me simply, 'Marquis.'"

The official again saluted and seizing Juve's valise traced on it the cabalistic chalk mark which allowed it to pass the frontier.

The evening before, the detective had taken his seat in the 10.50 express from the Gare du Nord in Paris for Cologne and Berlin. He had the good luck to find that a sleeping car had been attached to the end of the train which would take him directly to Glotzbourg. At the frontier he changed into a local, which jogged peacefully along, stopping every few minutes at small stations. The country of Hesse-Weimar spread out attractive and varied. Numerous small hills crowned with woods succeeded the green valleys they passed through. The houses were Swiss in architecture and seemed built for comfort and elegance. The little Kingdom seemed to breathe peace, simplicity and well-being. On his arrival at Hesse-Weimar, Juve had not been without some apprehension. During his last interview with Monsieur Annion he had put forward the opinion that an investigation in Hesse-Weimar would do much to clear up the mystery surrounding the affair. As a matter of fact, it was more to gain time than for any other reason that Juve had suggested this. He had not mentioned to his chief that his real object in going to Glotzbourg was to try to obtain a clue as to the real or apparent disappearance of the King Frederick-Christian II.

The formal declaration of the grotesque Wulf had reassured the French authorities as to the fate of the King, but to Juve, who knew that Fandor was installed at the Royal Palace, the search for the real King was of paramount importance.

"Glotzbourg.... All out!"

The detective seized his bag, hurried out of the car, hailed a cab and drove to the Hotel Deux-Hemispheres, which had been recommended by his colleague. After engaging his room Juve asked the porter to telephone to the police to find out when Heberlauf could see him. While waiting for the reply he took a bath and changed his clothes.

After having washed and shaved, he was about to go down to the lobby of the Hotel when a knock came at the door.

"Come in!" he cried.

A very tall and thin individual with a parchment-like face entered and bowed ceremoniously.

"To whom have I the honor...?" Juve inquired.

"I am Monsieur Heberlauf, head of the police at Hesse-Weimar....Have I the pleasure of speaking to Monsieur Juve?"

Juve, surprised at the visit, excused the disorder of the room and tried to make his guest comfortable.

"Monsieur Wulf advised me of your intended visit to our Capital."

In a very few moments Juve was able to size up his man, who seemed only too anxious to impart information about himself and his affairs. While quite as simple-minded as Wulf, he appeared far more sinister. Juve also divined without much difficulty that his wife, Madame Heloise Heberlauf, was the best informed woman in the kingdom regarding gossip and scandal.

"In fact," declared the chief of police, "I can be of very little assistance to you, Monsieur. But my wife can give you all the information you need."

Juve made it clear to Monsieur Heberlauf that he wished to obtain an entry to the Court as soon as possible.

Monsieur Heberlauf replied that nothing would be easier than a presentation to the Queen. It happened that she was receiving in the afternoon, and Madame Heberlauf would take the necessary steps for his introduction. He ended by saying:

"Do come and lunch with us without ceremony. You will have plenty of time afterward to dress for the reception.... Have you a Court costume?"

Juve had overlooked that item.

"No, I haven't," he replied. "Is it indispensable?"

"It is, but don't worry, Madame Heberlauf will take charge of that. She will be able to find you the necessary garments." The luncheon engagement made for twelve o'clock sharp, the Chief of Police, now more solemn than ever, rose and took his leave.

"Well, Monsieur Juve, don't you think that looks fine?"

Juve was anxiously regarding himself in the glass, examining the effect of his costume, while Madame Heberlauf, a fat little red-faced woman, was circling around, eyeing him from every angle and clapping her hands with pleasure at the success of her efforts.

The lunch had been bountiful, and thoroughly German. Preserved fruit was served with the fish, and gooseberry jam with the roast. Juve was now costumed in knee breeches and a dress coat which permitted him to enter the presence of royalty.

"Don't be late," Madame Heberlauf advised, "for the Queen is very punctual, and there are a number of formalities to go through before you can be presented to her."

The Palace of the King was on the outskirts of the town, and was reached by a drive through a Park which the inhabitants had named Pois de Pulugne. It was built upon the top of a hill and had a fine view over the surrounding country. The garden surrounding the Palace had been artistically laid out, a fine lawn stretching away from the main entrance. The building itself was a miniature copy of Versailles. Having left his carriage at the gate Juve followed Madame Heberlauf's instructions and made his way to the left wing of the Palace. Upon his card of introduction was written the title "Comte," for, as Madame Heberlauf had explained, the Queen had a penchant for meeting members of the nobility. "Your welcome will be made much easier if you are thought to be noble," Madame Heberlauf had explained. As it was imperative that the reason for Juve's visit should be kept from the Court, he had arranged a little story with Madame Heberlauf.

The Comte Juve was a Canadian explorer who, after a trip through Africa, was coming to spend some time at Glotzbourg and was anxious to meet the reigning family.

"God forgive us the lie," exclaimed Monsieur Heberlauf, "but as Monsieur Juve's mission is in the interest of the King Frederick-Christian, we are thoroughly justified in the deception."

The Queen's chamberlain, Monsieur Erick von Kampfen, after carefully examining Juve's credentials, led the detective into a drawing-room in which were already gathered a number of persons. An officer, in a wonderful uniform, came forward and introduced him to several of his companions.

"Princesse de Krauss, duc de Rutisheimer, colonel..."

Juve was not surprised at this. The excellent Madame Heberlauf had warned him that such was the usage of the Court, and that before being admitted to the presence of the sovereign, the guests were introduced to one another. Juve was on his guard against committing the slightest imprudence, but his new friends were quickly at ease with him and very amiable in their attentions. He was soon surrounded by a number of young women begging for details of his explorations. Among these people Juve picked out the Princesse de Krauss, a stout woman with exaggerated blonde hair and red spots on her face, barely disguised under a thick layer of powder. She seemed to be ready for a more personal conversation which Juve insensibly brought to bear upon the royal couple.

"Will His Majesty the King be present at the Queen's reception to-day?"

The Princess looked at Juve in amazement, and then burst out laughing.

"It is easy to see you have just arrived from the middle of Africa, or you would know that His Majesty the King is in Paris.... Surely you must know that, since you tell me that you came through Paris on your way here."

The Duchess de Rutisheimer, a rather pretty and distinguished looking woman, drew the detective apart and whispered behind her fan:

"Our King is a gay bird, Count, and we know very well why he goes to Paris."

The Duchess spoke with such an air of annoyance that Juve could hardly prevent a smile.

"One might criticise His Majesty for going so far away to seek what was so close to hand."

"Ah, indeed, you are right," the Princess sighed, "there must be something about these Parisian women. ... I heard that the dressmakers of the Rue de la Paix are going to bring out some Spring models which are so indecent..."

M. Erick von Kampfen, the chamberlain, entered the room at this moment and announced:

"Ladies and gentlemen, kindly pass into the gallery. Her Majesty the Queen will be ready to receive you in a moment."

Behind him came the little Duc Rudolphe, who was informing some of his friends as though it were a fine piece of scandal:

"The Grand Duchess Alexandra hasn't come yet ... and they are wondering if she will come."

CHAPTER XIV
QUEEN HEDWIGE RECEIVES

Obedient to the Grand Chamberlain's invitation, the assembled guests passed into the great gallery at the end of which an immense salon was seen, still empty; it was the room in which the Queen held her drawing-room.

It was sparsely furnished; a large gilded armchair, which was really a throne, stood at the farther end between two windows; the floor was waxed until it shone, and the surface was so slippery that Juve felt some fear of mishaps.

First came the guard with a clatter of sabres, then two heralds, and finally Her Majesty Hedwige, Queen of Hesse-Weimar, who proceeded to the throne and sat down.

She was a little body with a pinched and nervous expression of face. She trotted along like an old woman, her shoulders hunched up, and distributed nods right and left in response to the profound bows of her courtiers.

This was not in the least as Juve had pictured her. He had seen her a dozen years previously, when she was a young girl engaged to Frederick-Christian; she had then appeared charming, and majestic in bearing. Now she looked like a woman of the middle class, bourgeois from head to heels.

Near the throne stood two officers in gala uniform, while the guard formed a circle round the throne.

The audience began.

The first Chamberlain called out a name, and a matron, after making the three traditional courtseys, came forward and chatted in a low voice with the Queen. Juve was observing the ceremony with interest, when his reflections were cut short by a voice calling:

"Monsieur le Comte de Juff!"

The detective, slightly intimidated, advanced toward the sovereign, while the grand Chamberlain leaned over and whispered his name and rank to the Queen.

"Monsieur le Comte de Juff," said the Queen in a little tinkling voice, "I am very happy to meet you. I congratulate you upon your travels. I am especially interested in the natives of Africa. We had a negro village here a few years ago ... hadn't we, M. von Kampfen?"

"Quite true, your Majesty," replied the Chamberlain, bowing deeply. The Queen turned again to Juve:

"I congratulate you, Monsieur, and I beg you to persevere in the work to which your special aptitude calls you."

The interview was at an end, and Juve was left wondering whether he should leave the room. The Chamberlain signed to him to retire behind the throne, where he found the amiable Mme. Heberlauf.

Juve, now standing quite close to the Queen, was enabled to overhear the next interview; with an old professor this time — Professor Muller. The Queen said:

"I am very happy to meet you. I congratulate you upon your pupils. I am especially interested in scholars."

Then turning to the Chamberlain:

"We have some very excellent schools here, have we not, Monsieur Kampfen?"

"Quite true, your Majesty."

"I congratulate you. Can I beg you to persevere in the work to which your special aptitude calls you?"

It was all Juve could do to keep from bursting into laughter.

The same speech was being made to a couple of young girls who were making their début at the Court, when the circle round the Queen noticed that she was growing uneasy and pre-occupied. Finally she turned to her first maid of honor, and cried in a sharp tone:

"Really, Madame, it is extraordinary that the electric lights should have been turned on while it is still daylight!... Kindly see that they are extinguished."

The first maid of honor, very embarrassed, passed along the order to the second maid of honor, who in turn hunted up the lady of the household, who relaid the message to the captain of the guard, and while he went in search of the proper subordinate, the attention of the Court was distracted by the entrance of an individual to whom everybody paid the greatest deference.

The Chamberlain announced:

"His Highness, Prince Gudulfin!"

The Prince was a distinguished looking young man of twenty-five, clean-shaven and dressed with extreme care and richness of attire.

He presented a great contrast to his cousin, the Queen of Hesse-Weimar, and as he approached the throne, his head high and a sarcastic smile on his lips, Hedwige seemed to shrink into her armchair, unable to meet the look in his eyes.

The suppressed hatred of the reigning dynasty for the younger branch was of ancient date and a matter of common knowledge. The recent and prolonged absence of Frederick-Christian had given Prince Gudulfin the opportunity by which he had profited to advance his claims and conspire for the overthrow of the Government, with himself as the King of Hesse-Weimar.

Therefore his presence was regarded as a great piece of audacity, and every eye was watching how the Prince would be received. The question in every mind was whether the Grand Duchess Alexandra, a woman of majestic presence and great beauty, would also appear. Prince Gudulfin had been paying her conspicuous attentions, and it was rumored that the Duchess dreamed of a nobler crown than the one her rank gave her title to bear.

The appearance of the two at the Queen's reception! What a scandal! But with the presence of the Prince came definite word that the Duchess had excused herself on the ground of a severe headache, a pretext which deceived nobody.

Prince Gudulfin, after observing the correct formalities, stood before the Queen waiting for the invitation to sit by her side.

Hedwige, still preoccupied by the electric lights, seemed to have forgotten him, and the situation was fast becoming embarrassing for the Prince, who could neither go nor stay. It was not long, however, before he saw what was troubling the Queen, and stepping aside he turned off the lights.

"There is no such thing as unnecessary economy, is there, cousin?" he murmured with a smile.

Hedwige blushed and gave him a furious look. She then proffered the tardy invitation to sit by her side. As the audience came to a close, the Queen in a loud voice announced:

"I wish to inform you that I have received news of the King. His Majesty is well and is in Paris. He will return very soon."

The Queen's guard now led the way back to the private apartments, followed by the maids of honor, and then the Queen herself hurried off as though glad to be finished with the whole affair.

Juve, an attentive listener to the numberless intrigues on foot on every side, divined the comedies and tragedies which underlay this little Court, more gossipy and vulgar than a servant's parlor. Especially he noted the frequent and bitter allusions to the perpetual trips of the King to Paris. These cost the royal treasury a pretty penny, and for the twentieth time Juve heard references to a certain red diamond belonging to Frederick-Christian. He had known for a long time that such a diamond was numbered among the crown jewels, and that it was supposed to represent a value of several millions, but he had imagined it was kept in a place of safety. Now he learned that the King was suspected of having pawned it to raise money. With his most innocent air, he questioned one of the officers.

"I should think it a very simple matter to find out whether the King took the diamond with him. It must surely be in the keeping of loyal and tried officials."

The officer smiled:

"My dear Count, it is easily seen that you come from the depths of Africa. Otherwise you would know that the diamond is hidden in the private apartments of the King — nobody knows where, not even the Queen. You may easily divine the uneasiness of the people and the advantage the affair gives to Prince Gudulfin."

Juve now felt that the King was still in Paris. The problem thus far had become clearer. But under what conditions was he living? It was quite possible that he had been kidnapped by some person who knew of the diamond's existence.

While pondering these matters, Juve had unconsciously wandered away from the salon and now found himself in the ante-room on the ground floor. Here he came face to face with Mme. Heberlauf, who was accompanied by a white-haired old man whom she at once introduced.

"Count de Juff, let me present the Dean of the Court, the Burgomaster of Rung Cassel..."

"The deuce!" thought Juve, "a bore, by the look of him!"

Escape was hopeless, the Burgomaster seized the detective by the arm and announced:

"I am the author of a work in 25 volumes on "The History of the Dark Continent." Now I hear that you have just returned from a journey of exploration in Africa and..."

The old historian dragged Juve into the Palace gardens and the latter thought:

"Hang it, I couldn't have pitched on a worse introduction, I don't know the first thing about Africa."

But the author of the 25 volumes quickly set him at ease. For he began by admitting that he himself had never set foot out of Glotzbourg.

Under these circumstances Juve recovered his nerve and glibly discussed the peculiarities of the African fauna.

An hour later the two men were still talking, but this time it was Juve who was anxious to keep the conversation going. The good Burgomaster had drifted into gossip about the affairs of the Kingdom; suddenly he turned to the detective with a question:

"Do you believe in this story about a visit to Paris?"

Juve hesitated and then made an ambiguous reply.

The Burgomaster continued:

"Personally, I don't. You see, my windows look toward the large octagonal wing in which are the apartments of the King. Now, for the past week I have noticed strange lights moving about in these supposedly empty rooms, and I have a notion that our dear King Frederick-Christian is very far from being in Paris. In fact, I think he is held a prisoner in his own Palace!

"Ah, Monsieur, you cannot imagine the intrigues which are being hatched against that noble heart; the black wickedness of the soul of Prince Gudulfin, hidden under the exterior of his seductive person!"

Juve was impressed. He was inclined to give some credence to the suppositions of the Burgomaster. For, after all, his search in Paris for the King had been without result and he had had the presentiment that his trip to Hesse-Weimar would throw some light upon the strange disappearance of the monarch.

So, while the old man was talking, Juve carefully noted in his mind the minutest architectural details of the octagonal tower which stood out clearly against the sky.

CHAPTER XV
THE MYSTERIOUS PRISON

"Good Lord! How my head aches! It feels as though it were made of lead!...I have a fire in my veins and such a thirst! Here and now I make a firm resolution never to give way again to such dissipation. Never again will I drink champagne in such quantities. But, where the deuce am I?...It's still pitch dark!...Ah, I remember ...it's outrageous! Help! Help!"

King Frederick-Christian had wakened. At first he experienced the usual unpleasant sensations which follow a night of heavy drinking and then, as his memory returned, he was afraid, horribly afraid.

He recalled his arrival at Susy d'Orsel's apartment in company with the young companion he had picked up at Raxim's and the subsequent supper, and then he broke into a cold sweat as his mind flashed to the picture of Fandor's return with the inanimate body of his mistress in his arms — dead. Yes, she was undoubtedly dead!

And afterwards, what had happened?

His companion had declared himself to be the journalist, Jerome Fandor, and had called him by name — Frederick-Christian. Furthermore, he had cried:

"It was you who killed Susy d'Orsel. It was you who threw her out of the window!"

What had happened after that? His mind was a complete blank.

Had these events occurred recently, or a long time ago? His headache and thirst were proof that they could not have been far distant.

"Where am I? Evidently not at the Royal Palace!"

When he first wakened he was lying flat on his back; now he sat up and groped about with his hands. The ground beneath him was cold and hard ...a floor of earth. So they had put him in a vault? in a cellar?

The air he breathed was heavy and warm, and the walls of his cell felt damp to the touch. Could he be in prison? That was hardly possible, in such a short time. Besides, he was innocent! As he sat listening, he detected a faint and faraway rumbling sound. It seemed to come from above his head.

As his senses became more fully aroused, an indefinable terror struck to his heart. At all costs he must take some action. He rose suddenly to his feet but before he reached his full height his head struck the roof. The blow was so violent that he fell back again in a fainting condition.

It was not until many hours afterward that he regained his senses sufficiently to make another attempt. This time he proceeded with more caution.

"I am the victim of some gang," he thought. "This Jerome Fandor is probably the leader of a band of cutthroats who, after killing Susy d'Orsel, took advantage of my intoxication to make me unconscious with some narcotic, and then dragged me to the place I am now in."

The King now began to explore the place on his hands and knees, his ears keenly alive to the slightest sound. He crawled around trying to discover the extent and nature of his prison.

The floor appeared to be of hard earth with occasional stretches of cement. The walls were smooth, but whether of stone or metal he could not determine. The height of the ceiling at the point where he lay was not over three feet, but gradually rose, vault-like, until he was able to stand fully upright. Was he buried alive in some kind of tomb? The idea terrified him and he began to shout for help. After many fruitless efforts and completely exhausted, he dropped to the ground overcome with the horror of his situation.

The distant rumbling sound now became louder from time to time, and at moments shook the walls of his prison, then died away to a faint murmur.

Frederick-Christian now tried to collect his thoughts upon the situation and bring some sort of order to his mind.

Susy d'Orsel was dead...

The King had felt no deep love for the girl. Still, he had been fond of her in a way and her sudden death affected him deeply.

He himself was a prisoner. But a prisoner of whom? Evidently of those who had killed his mistress. Again, in all probability, they did not contemplate killing him since they had had the opportunity to do so and he was still alive and unharmed. This being so, they would not let him die of hunger and thirst.

His watch had stopped and he had no way of measuring the lapse of time; but his attention was called to the fact that the rumbling noises were happening at greater intervals.

"The pulse-beats of a man are separated by intervals of a second," he thought, "and by counting my pulse I can determine the interval between the rumbling, and thus gain some idea of the passing hours."

He was about to put this plan into practice when a sudden cry escaped him:

"Good God!"

In the blackness of his cell a thin shaft of light appeared.

The King sprang toward it, but found the light too feeble for him to distinguish surrounding objects by. It entered the cell through a small fissure in one of the walls, and after a few minutes was suddenly withdrawn. Frederick-Christian stumbled forward in the darkness and, after taking a few steps, his feet struck some object lying on the ground. Stooping down, he groped with his hands until they touched something that drew from him an exclamation of joy ... he had found a pile of bottles. He seized one and opened it with a corkscrew which lay near by.

One draught and he realized that the bottle contained wine. Thereupon he opened several more but with the same result. To drink them would only increase his thirst. He had the strength to resist the temptation. Again he moved forward and this time ran into a large box. His hand touched something cold. It was meat of some kind. After smelling and tasting it he flung it from him. It was a salt ham.

Hours passed while Frederick-Christian suffered the tortures of hunger and thirst. Cold and tired out, he finally lay down on the ground, writhing with violent pains in his stomach. At length he could stand it no longer, and dragging himself to the box, he seized the ham and began to devour it ravenously. This brought on a maddening thirst, which he tried to quench by long draughts of the wine. Then he became very drunk and so, laughing and crying, he drank until he lost consciousness once more.

"Sire! Can you hear me?"

A sharp voice broke the silence. It seemed to come from a distance.

"Sire, can you hear me?... Answer!"

Frederick-Christian sprang up.

"Who is speaking? Who are you? Help! Help!"

The voice, mocking and authoritative, answered:

"Now, then, keep quiet. I am not within reach, so it is useless to cry for help."

"Scoundrel!" cried the King.

"There's no use in behaving like a child ...you won't gain anything by it."

"Pity, pity!...I will make you rich ...I will give you anything you ask, only set me at liberty ... take me out of this prison or I shall become mad."

"Have you done with your lamentations?"

"I'll be revenged!"

"I am beyond your vengeance, Sire, and you would do well to talk quietly with me."

"You killed my mistress, Susy d'Orsel!"

"Yes, I killed her."

"You are Fandor — Jerome Fandor!"

"What you say is absurd."

"And my Kingdom? The Queen, my wife? What is happening?"

"I didn't come here to discuss politics with you. You must be reasonable."

"What do you want with me? Why was I brought here?"

"Ah, now we can discuss the matter together. You ask me what I want. First of all, let me reassure you. I do not intend to kill you. Your death would not be of the slightest use to me. Otherwise I shouldn't hesitate an instant."

"I'm not afraid of death."

"I know that, Sire …you are brave.…I want your diamond."

"My diamond!"

"Exactly. I am quite aware, Frederick-Christian, that your personal fortune is represented by a diamond of marvelous purity and size. I also know that it is hidden in your Palace. You, alone, know where. I want you to disclose its hiding place to me so that I may go and get it."

"Never! I'm not a coward!"

"You are stupid, Sire. I repeat, once in possession of the diamond, I will set you at liberty."

"Lies!"

"Sire, consider a moment. It would be practically impossible for me to realize anything like the value of the diamond. To sell it I should be obliged to break it into small pieces, and in that case it would scarcely fetch more than twenty millions. Now, I have a better suggestion to offer."

"What is it?"

"You are to give me directions how to find it. Once in my possession, you are free. You will then draw the sum of fifty millions from your bank. As King that will be quite possible. This money you will turn over to me in exchange for your diamond. And don't think you will be able to catch me. I shall take care that the exchange is made without witnesses, and in such a way that I run no risk of arrest. Now, what do you say to my proposition?"

"I refuse."

"Very well, then in two hours you will be dead. I pledge my word for it.…And my word has some value. Perhaps you guess who I am."

"Who? Who?"

"I am Fantômas, Sire."

At this name of horror and crime, Frederick-Christian was seized with the utmost terror. In a broken voice he replied:

"I accept."

And then in trembling, disjointed sentences, he gave up the secret of the hiding place in his Palace at Glotzbourg.

CHAPTER XVI
THE THEFT OF THE DIAMOND

Queen Hedwige had had a serious and legitimate reason for bringing her reception to an abrupt conclusion. A Court ball for the high functionaries and dignities of the Kingdom was to take place that evening.

Furthermore, the Queen was very much exercised over the rumor that the Grand Duchess Alexandra was to be present. This woman, still young and very beautiful, played an important rôle in the small world of the Palace. It was said by the gossips that she accepted the attentions of Prince Gudulfin, in the hope that some day she might share the throne of Hesse-Weimar with him. For many years she had been a great traveler but in recent times she had spent more and more of her time in Glotzbourg, where she continually met the Prince.

While Juve had experienced no difficulty in being present at the Queen's audience, he found that even Mme. Heberlauf's influence was not sufficient to procure him an invitation to the ball. As a matter of fact, he had no particular wish to appear in the quality of a guest that evening. He had other plans.

At ten o'clock a long line of carriages and automobiles began to arrive in the gardens of the Palace. Innumerable electric lights shone out along the drive-way and from the windows. A few persons had managed to slip past the guards and had stationed themselves near the awning at the main entrance to watch the arrival of the guests. Beneath their fur cloaks, the women wore their very finest gowns and their richest jewelry.

The hall of the chancellory had been transformed into a cloakroom and there the crowd was thickest. In contrast to the brilliantly illuminated left wing of the château, the octagonal tower showed dark and silent. Hiding behind pillars, keeping close to the walls, a man was making his way slowly toward that tower.

The man was Juve.

From behind a big tree he stood and watched the sky, rubbing his hands with satisfaction.

"This is a night after my own heart," he murmured, "overcast and dark. I should have been very embarrassed had the moon come out."

He felt his pockets.

"Everything I need. My electric lamp and a good, strong, silk ladder."

Then, surveying the tower, he soliloquized:

"A fine monument! Solid and strong. They don't build them like that nowadays."

Juve took a few steps, bent his knees and stretched his arms, tested the suppleness of his body.

"Ah, in spite of my forty-odd years, I'm still pretty fit for ... the work I have to do."

By the aid of the lightning rod, the gutters and the inequalities in the stones, the detective was enabled to climb without much difficulty to the first floor.

There he paused to take breath and to examine the shutters of a window.

"Can't get in that way," he muttered, "they're bolted inside. I'll have to climb higher."

The same condition met him on the second floor, but when he had finally reached the roof, he espied a large chimney which promised a method of ingress to the apartment below. The descent was anything but easy, and Juve, in spite of his great strength and agility, was used up by the time he had reached the bottom. His clothes were torn and he was covered with the greasy soot he had accumulated on his journey. By dint of brushing and scraping, he succeeded in cleaning off the worst of it, and then looked round to take his bearings.

He had landed in the large waiting-room which adjoined the royal apartments.

The distant sound of dance music came to his ears and the atmosphere of the place was cold and damp.

"He doesn't often come here, I'll bet," thought Juve.

A door led him directly into the King's bathroom, and Juve paused to admire the famous bath of solid silver which the municipality had presented to the King upon one of his birthdays.

"I've a good mind to take a tub," he muttered. "Maybe I shall find His Majesty locked in his bedroom, and I'm hardly a fit sight to appear before him."

The detective now felt some cause for anxiety.

There were two alternatives to consider. Either the King was absent, and in that case Juve's business would be to discover the hiding place of the diamond and clear up the question whether the King had taken it with him, or, if he had been sequestered, to discover his prison.

Clutching the butt of his Browning revolver in his pocket, the detective opened the door to the King's bedroom and entered.

A thick carpet deadened the sound of his footsteps. After listening for a few moments he relit his pocket lamp and flashed it round the room.

In the centre stood an immense bed of oak designed in Renaissance style, the posts of which reached to the ceiling. Three steps led up to it. Juve noticed that it had not been disturbed. The sheets and pillows were all in order. There was nothing, however, to indicate that the King had been absent for any length of time.

Upon one point he was certain: The King was not concealed anywhere about the room, and the more he thought of the Burgomaster's suspicion, the less he thought it plausible. But if the King had not been sequestered, it was quite possible that he might be purposely hiding after his unfortunate adventure of the Rue de Monceau. Therefore, Juve decided to pursue his search through the other rooms.

But first he began mechanically to tap the wood-work, looking behind the pictures for the hiding place of the famous diamond. In his time he had seen so many secret drawers, double-seated chairs, and numerous contrivances of a similar sort, that it would be a cunning hand that could baffle his perspicacity and experience.

He had just examined a chair when suddenly he stopped in his work and waited, listening. The sound of footsteps some distance off struck his ear. Without a moment's hesitation he put out his light and darted behind the curtains. It was a good position to take up for he could see without being seen.

The footsteps drew near, the door opened and a light from an electric lantern similar to the one Juve had used, was thrown into the room.

The individual advanced to the bed, all unaware of Juve's presence. Stooping down, he began feeling the foot of one of the bedposts, which at this point formed a bulge. In an instant the wood parted and disclosed a hollow in which lay a jewel case. The jewel case contained the famous red diamond.

Juve's heart began to thump as he watched the man open the case and take out the diamond. Its facets reflected the light, multiplying the gleams and bringing into relief the features of the robber.

Then it was that the detective uttered a great cry, a cry of agony, of anger and of triumph. The man was wrapped in a great cloak, his face hidden by a black mask, but there was no mistaking his identity. It was Fantômas.

Juve's cry called forth another, ferocious and menacing, and then in a moment the room was plunged into darkness and the two men sprang at one another. Two revolver shots rang out. The dancers heard them in the ballroom and stopped dancing. The musicians heard them and ceased playing.

At once a stampede ensued.

Two officers of the guard rushed to the door leading to the King's apartments, and flung it wide open. One of them turned on the electric light and, followed by the frightened guests, entered the King's bedchamber.

At the foot of the bed, struggling in a long cloak, a man with his hands over his face lay moaning. By his side was a smoking revolver, and on the ground the empty jewel case.

"Arrest him!" somebody cried.

In a moment a number of hands had seized and bound him. It was noticed that his eyelids were fearfully swollen and the eyes bloodshot.

What had happened!

The struggle between Juve and the monster had scarcely lasted a second.

The detective had fired point blank at the black mask and as his finger pressed the trigger he had felt the whistle of a bullet past his ear.

Then a door had opened slightly, letting in a thin shaft of light. To his amazement, Fantômas no longer stood before him, but an officer in the uniform of the Queen's lancers.

Juve was not taken in by this quick change, and was on the point of firing again when suddenly his eyes were filled with a blinding powder, burning and blistering the pupils. He had been blinded by pepper. Instinctively he put his hands to his face, and in that moment he felt himself enveloped in the long cloak in which Fantômas had entangled him. Falling to the ground in agony he then heard the cry:

"Help! Help!"

By the sudden and growing noise, he realized that the crowd was drawing near. When he had struggled to a sitting posture, he found himself a prisoner.

The sudden change from darkness to bright light increased the pain in his eyes, but with a superhuman effort he was enabled to pick out the superb uniform of the false lancer. Pointing to him, he cried:

"Arrest him, why don't you arrest him!"

Brutally, he was told to keep quiet.

The noise of the theft spread rapidly and the greatest confusion reigned in the Palace. Many of the women fainted. Finally M. Heberlauf arrived. He appeared immensely important, and confided to a group his opinion of the affair, adding this restriction:

"At any rate, that is what my wife believes."

Mme. Heberlauf had, in fact, after an interview with one of the officers, announced it as her opinion that the thief so providentially arrested was no other than the world-famous and unseizable Fantômas.

And then a queer thing happened. When the Grand Duchess Alexandra heard this sinister name spoken, when she knew that Fantômas had been arrested, she staggered as though struck to the heart and fell fainting into the arms of her friends.

"Fantômas!" she murmured, "Fantômas arrested! Can it be possible?"

Juve was taken away tightly bound. He seemed indifferent to the clamor of the crowd and constantly looked from side to side as though searching for something or somebody. Suddenly, as he passed the group surrounding the Grand Duchess Alexandra, he made a violent effort and dragged his captors close enough to enable him to see the fainting woman's features. One look was enough, and then without further resistance he allowed himself to be marched away. He had found out what he wanted to know; he had recognized in the Grand Duchess the mistress of Fantômas, the accomplice of his most dreadful crimes. He had seen Lady Beltham!

CHAPTER XVII
ON THE RIGHT TRAIL

"The Bureau of Public Highways, if you please?"

"What is it you wish to inquire about?"

"I want some information as to the probable duration of certain repair works."

"Ah, then go to the fourth floor, number 54, door to the right at the end of the passage."

"Thanks."

With a slight nod, the visitor entered the huge building on the Boulevard Saint-Germain, which houses the offices of Public Works. He was a young man, dressed in a long black overcoat, a derby hat, which he wore well down over his eyes, and a wide bandage that covered one eye and part of the cheek.

After climbing the four flights indicated, he discovered that he had evidently taken the wrong staircase. There was nothing to do then but to go back to the porter's lodge and get more explicit instructions. But after taking a few steps, he hesitated.

"Fandor, old chap," he soliloquized, "what's the use of showing yourself and taking the risk of being recognized as the erstwhile King of Hesse-Weimar?"

For the individual who was in search of the Bureau of Public Works was no other than the journalist. An hour previously he had succeeded by clever strategy in getting rid of the excellent Wulf, who was at all times very loath to let the King out of his sight. Then, rushing to his own apartment, he had changed his clothes and partly covered his face with the bandage to conceal his features.

After several futile attempts, aided by innumerable directions from passing employés, he at length reached the office of which he was in search. There he encountered a clerk who viewed him with a suspicious eye.

"What do you want, Monsieur?"

"I want some information."

"We don't give information here."

"Really!... Why not?"

"Are you a contractor?"

"No."

"You wish to lodge a complaint?"

"No."

"Then what is your business?"

"Just to get some information as to the probable duration of certain works."

"You are not a reporter?"

"I am not a reporter. I am an advertising agent."

"Ah, that's different. The office you are looking for is number 43, the door opposite ... but there's nobody in now. However, you can wait."

Fandor crossed and entered room 43, where, after a moment, he discovered an occupant tucked away behind an enormous pile of books and manuscripts. This clerk was absorbed in a yellow-covered novel and greeted Fandor with evident ill-humor.

"What d'you want?"

"I would like to know, Monsieur, the probable duration of the repair work in operation at the Place de la Concorde."

"And why do you want to know that?"

"I am an advertising agent, and I may have a proposition to offer to the city."

"And at what point is this work in operation?"

"At the corner of the wall of the Orangery and the Quay."

After consulting a large register, the clerk turned to Fandor, shutting the book with a bang.

"Nothing is being done there. You are mistaken."

"But I've just come from there. There is a ditch and a palisade."

"No, no, no such thing. In every quarter of Paris the police are obliged to notify me of any public works in operation, and an entry is made in my register to that effect. Now, I have no record of the repairs you speak of, consequently they don't exist."

Fandor left the office, hailed a cab and ordered the driver to take him to the National Library.

"Hang it," he muttered, "I saw the ditch and the palisade myself! Now, if they are not the work of the city, it will be interesting to find out what is going on there....Ah! suppose this idiot Wulf was not deceived! Suppose he really heard the Singing Fountains the other evening giving the last bars of the national hymn of Hesse-Weimar!"

Arrived at the National Library, Fandor began a long and minute search through volumes on architecture, on statuary and a multitude of guide books to Paris! He was so engrossed in his work that when four o'clock struck he sprang up suddenly.

"Good heavens! I've scarcely time to get back to my apartment, change into my kingly clothes and meet Wulf, to become once more His Majesty Frederick-Christian!"

In his apartment in his own house, the extraordinary Marquis de Sérac, who was also the common Mme. Ceiron, was whispering to a person hidden behind the curtains.

"You understand, don't move and listen with all your ears, and promise me not to interfere until I give you permission!"

"I promise. Monsieur le Marquis," replied the individual in a low tone.

"All right, then I'll have her in."

The Marquis crossed the room and opened a door.

"Come in, Mademoiselle, and forgive me for keeping you waiting. I had visitors."

"Oh, Monsieur," replied Marie Pascal, for it was the young seamstress, "don't mention it ... and let me thank you for your recommendation to the King. I got two big orders from it."

"Oh, I was very glad to be of service to you with Frederick-Christian....I regret only one thing, Mademoiselle, and that is the unhappy events which have clouded His Majesty's visit to Paris."

"Yes, indeed," replied Marie Pascal, "and in such a tragic way, too!"

"A tragic way, Mademoiselle? I imagine this has quite upset you."

"Yes."

The Marquis emphasized his words.

"So I thought, so I thought ... especially you."

The young girl lifted her pure blue eyes in surprise.

"The King spoke to me of you at great length," the Marquis added.

A quick blush overspread her face.

"Really....The King spoke of me?"

"His Majesty told me you were charming. He noticed you the very first time you went to see him."

"At the Royal Palace?...But he only got a glimpse of me through the open door."

The Marquis smiled.

"Oh, it doesn't take long for a King ... or a young man to sometimes dream of the impossible."

"Impossible ... yes, you are right."

Marie Pascal pronounced the last words in a serious voice. She was making an evident effort to keep calm. The Marquis, on the other hand, seemed inclined to joke.

"Impossible, why?...One never knows ... the will of the King knows no obstacle." Then brusquely turning, he asked:

"You like the King, Mademoiselle?"

"Why ... why..."

"Therefore, I'm wondering if the death of this unfortunate Susy is not really a benefit."

"Oh, Monsieur!"

"Well, you know, Mademoiselle Marie, the happiness of one person is made of the tears of another. You would have suffered. You would have been jealous."

As though against her will, Marie Pascal repeated in a low voice:

"Yes, I should have been jealous."

"Terribly jealous, for Susy d'Orsel was pretty. Besides, a liaison with her wasn't taken seriously by the King ...while with you it would have been quite different ...why, I believe you would have reached the point of wishing her death."

"No! no!" protested Marie feebly, "the King would have made his choice ...frankly and loyally...."

"And suppose he hadn't chosen? Suppose he had hesitated before the possible scandal of a rupture? Don't you care enough for him to realize that the very idea of sharing him with another would have been intolerable?...What I am saying sounds brutal, I know, but I am frank with you....Believe me, you would have been driven to hate the unfortunate Susy."

"To hate her? Yes, ...perhaps ...for I should have been jealous!"

And then suddenly Marie realized what her words meant: that she had betrayed her cherished secret ...her love. In a moment she burst into sobs and collapsed on the sofa.

The Marquis de Sérac very gently tried to reassure her.

"Don't cry, my poor child. After all, you are lamenting imaginary misfortunes which I have so imprudently imagined....They don't exist, and never could exist, for it is a fact that Susy d'Orsel is no longer a rival to be feared. Think rather of the future which smiles upon you. You love and you have some reason to hope that you are loved in return, so dry your eyes ... fate has withdrawn the one obstacle which existed between you and the King."

Tremblingly, Marie Pascal rose.

"Forgive me, Monsieur, for this stupid scene. I lost my self ...control....I confessed a feeling which I should have kept a secret....I'm so confused I no longer know what I'm saying ...so please let me go."

The Marquis, with exquisite politeness, opened the door for her.

"Promise to come and see me again, Mademoiselle; before long I shall probably have something further of interest to say to you."

When the door had closed upon Marie Pascal, the Marquis drew aside the portières.

"Come out, my dear fellow....We shall be alone now!"

Wulf appeared. A Wulf literally armed to the teeth, and ready for any emergency.

"Put up your arsenal, we are in no danger," exclaimed the Marquis, "and tell me what you think of the visit."

"I think there is not a moment to lose," replied Wulf, agitated. "She loves the King and she hated Susy d'Orsel, therefore she is the assassin. She is the cause of all the troubles that have fallen upon the head of our beloved sovereign. Ah! I want to arrest her! Condemn her to death! Come, Marquis, let us go to her room and seize her!"

"Not yet a while, Wulf; sit down and talk it over. To begin with, we can arrest nobody without proof ...presumption is not sufficient."

"I'll force her to confess!"

"You wouldn't succeed, Wulf, and besides, you have no power to arrest her yourself. That is work for the French authorities. Your duty is simply to go and warn Juve."

"Right away! At once!"

"Hold on ...remember, you are to do nothing without my permission. Now, I repeat, we have no proof yet to offer ...but listen carefully, for I have a plan ...this is it...."

Two hours later, Wulf rejoined Fandor in a boulevard café. The excellent man had such an air of elation that the journalist wondered:

"What fool thing is this idiot getting ready to do now!"

CHAPTER XVIII
A SLEEPER

Fandor sat up in bed as the door of his room opened to admit the cautious head of Wulf. "Your Majesty is awake?" he inquired.

"Yes, my Majesty is awake and ready to get up. Wulf, we are going out to-day."

"As your Majesty wishes."

"The Queen has written to say that she is getting bored, and wants me home again. That being the case we had better make the most of our few remaining days, you understand?"

"Not very well."

"Why, this afternoon we must look up some pretty girls and, as my cousin the King of England says, 'Honi soit qui mal y pense.' Evil to him who evil thinks. And now, au revoir, my dear Wulf; by and by I'll invite you to crack a bottle with me."

The punctilious Wulf made the three bows demanded by etiquette, turned on his heel, and left the room.

Fandor sprang out of bed and began to dress.

"After all, it's not altogether a joke," he muttered. "I had to listen to that idiot Wulf jawing away all yesterday evening ... and if I remember right, he said something about being suspicious of that little Marie Pascal. I'll have to stop him making more blunders. He's quite capable of having her arrested. Anyway, Wulf is to do nothing till the return of Juve, and that will give me time to take my precautions."

Fandor and Wulf had just finished a very excellent dinner, which Fandor paid for out of his own pocket. He was careful not to take any of the royal funds for his personal use. Wulf hovered on the borderland of drunkenness, but his ideas still showed some coherence. For the twentieth time he asked Fandor the same question:

"But, Sire, why the deuce are you wearing a false moustache and whiskers to-day?"

"So that I may not be recognized, my friend. I don't like having to give royal tips everywhere."

Fandor was not speaking the truth. His disguise was assumed for other reasons. He did not wish to be recognized either as Frederick-Christian or as Fandor. Since noon — and it was now ten o'clock at night — the two men had been doing Paris together, and Wulf had received the very gratifying appellations of "my excellent friend," "my subtle detective," and other flattering names, so he was now dreaming of decorations, new decorations created especially for him.

Fandor interrupted his thoughts by patting him familiarly on the shoulder:

"Now that we've had dinner, I'm going to tell you something. We've had quite a day of it; we've visited the Bois, where you spat in the lake, the action of a reflective mind; we've been to the top of the Arc de Triomphe and to the Madeleine, so now there is only one joy remaining."

Wulf nodded: "To pay for the dinner."

"Not exactly," laughed Fandor, "that's more of a penance. No, I was referring to a chance meeting, a charming feminine figure, a kiss, a caress. Wulf, what would you say to two plump white arms around your neck?"

Wulf became purple in the face.

"Oh, Sire, that would be great! But when I am with your Majesty, I don't look at women."

"And why not, Wulf?"

"Because the women only look at you."

"That's so, Wulf, that's so; but there is a way of fixing that. You order a drink which I will pay for, then sit here and count all the carriages that pass in the street while I do an errand, it will only take twenty-five minutes....I'm going to see a girl I know you understand?"

"Yes, Sire. Must I count all the carriages?"

"No, only those drawn by white horses. Au revoir, Wulf."

Fandor left the café and hailed a cab:

"Rue Bonaparte. I'll tell you where to stop." He settled back in his seat, an anxious frown on his face.

"I'll just drop a hint to Juve," he thought. "One never knows what may happen....I suppose he'll be back soon ... to-morrow morning or evening ... and won't he be glad to hear the result of my search!"

Fandor tapped on the glass with his cane, got out, paid the driver and made his way to the house where Juve lived. He still had his pass-key and let himself in, calling:

"Hello! Juve, are you in?"

There was no answer, so Fandor sat at Juve's desk and wrote a long letter, then tracing a diagram upon another sheet, he put them into an envelope addressed to "Monsieur Juve — Urgent."

When he rejoined Wulf, he found the faithful detective on his job.

"I've counted up to 99, Sire, but I'm not quite sure that I'm exact. A bay horse passed, and I wasn't sure whether to count him or not."

"That's all right, we'll take this up another time. I've spoken of you to my little friend and she is crazy to meet you, Wulf."

"Oh, Sire! Sire!"

"Yes ... so come along."

"To her house?"

"Oh, no — this lady is poetic, she wants the first meeting to take place in appropriate surroundings."

While Wulf was cudgeling his brains to think up a verse or two to fit the occasion, Fandor guided him down the Rue Castiglione, the Rue de Rivoli and at length reached the Place de la Concorde. He cast an anxious glance as he passed at the mysterious repairs, repairs not indexed by the administration, and then turned to the Singing Fountains.

"Sire, is this the place?"

"Yes, Wulf, but first there are a few formalities to be gone through."

The two men had reached the parapet overlooking the Seine.

"You are to stand here, Wulf, and look down at the water. You are not to take your eyes off it."

"Why? What does your Majesty mean?"

"Because I have a surprise in store for you, and also I wish to bring about the meeting in a natural manner — to spare the lady's feelings. Now I shall go to meet her and take her to the Singing Fountains. When I whistle you are to join us. Does that meet with your approval?"

"Your Majesty is most kind."

Fandor moved away and after glancing back to make sure Wulf was obeying orders, he quickly drew his revolver and approached the works.

"I must remember Juve's precept," he muttered, "never fire first, and then only when you're sure to hit."

The journalist now examined the palisade which surrounded a ditch of some depth dug in the angle made by the Orangery walls.

"Can't see anything from the outside," he thought, "so I'll go in."

With a running jump he succeeded in catching hold of the palisade top and in a moment was sitting astride of it.

Nobody was in sight. Fandor was a little surprised. He expected to be confronted by some sinister individual.

"All right," he growled, "if you don't mind I'll come in."

Letting go of the top he slid down to the ground. There he found a large hole in which was placed a ladder. This led to the bottom of the ditch where a series of pipes protruded from the soil. Fandor lit his pocket lamp and carefully examined the surroundings.

"Ah," he exclaimed, "it looks as though some perfectly natural repair work was going on."

He then went down listening at each pipe mouth. One of them gave out a peculiar sound, steady and cadenced, in fact, a snore, a real snore.

"Can he be asleep," he muttered.

Climbing quickly out of the ditch, Fandor reached the street again and ran toward the Singing Fountains.

"Either the 'Curiosities of Paris' which I read yesterday in the library is a collection of bad jokes, or the body of the third statue..."

He did not complete his thought.

After once more making sure that nobody was about, and that the excellent Wulf was still absorbed in contemplation of the Seine, he climbed into the basin at the foot of one of the bronze naiads and waded through mud and water to the base of the statue.

"Now, then, let's see, what must I do next? Seize the statue by the neck, place the left hand in the middle of the body and sway it."

Suiting the action to the word, the journalist applied all his force and in a moment the statue parted in two and swung toward him. The hollow interior appeared like a black hole. Bending forward, Fandor cried:

"Sire, Sire, can you hear me?"

His voice came echoing back to him, but there was no reply from the depths.

"Ah, I can't be mistaken!" he cried, desperately. "Wulf heard this fountain singing the national anthem of Hesse-Weimar, the statue is hollow, therefore the King should be hidden in it."

Again he stood, listening. After a pause an exclamation of surprise escaped him.

"Why, it's the same noise I heard in the pipe ... it's a snore ... the unfortunate man is somewhere asleep!"

To call louder would have been dangerous, and besides, quick action was necessary.

"Nothing venture, nothing gain," he whispered, as, revolver in hand, he stepped inside the statue. He slid rapidly down for a distance of six or eight feet and then landed on earth. There he lay for a minute or two, reasoning that if he should be met by a fusillade, he would be safer in that position.

However, complete silence reigned about him, broken only by the steady and distant snoring.

Then, lighting his electric lamp, Fandor began a survey of the premises into which he had so daringly intruded.

CHAPTER XIX
FREE!

After a brief inspection, a cry of surprise rose to his lips.

"Good Lord!...there he is! Frederick-Christian."

It was indeed the King — a prisoner in the hollow foundations of the Singing Fountains.

"Sire, Sire!"

The King slept on. But his sleep seemed troubled; he breathed in gasps.

"Sire! Sire! Wake up! I have come to save you! Upon my word, that is what might be called a royal sleep."

The journalist's words made no impression on the sleeping monarch, so, ignoring all formality, he laid hands upon the King and gave him a violent shaking.

"For Heaven's sake, try to recognize me ...speak to me ...I am Jerome Fandor ...I've come to save you."

In leaning over the sleeping man, Fandor suddenly got a whiff of his breath and then drew back, amazed.

"Why, he's drunk! As drunk as a lord! Where the deuce did he get it?...Ah, these empty bottles!...Wine!...and ham ...no wonder! What on earth shall I do with him now? How can I get him out of here? I can't leave him in the hands of the cutthroats who have imprisoned him....But if I do take him away, how the devil will Juve and I be able to catch the accomplices of Fantômas, if he has any?"

"Juve!"

The very name of the detective gave him an inspiration.

"Yes, that's the only way out of it ...first of all, I must save the King, get him out of danger, and then arrange a trap to catch my gang." Fandor deliberated a moment.

"There's no doubt I shall run the risk of being killed in his place, but that's a risk I shall have to take."

And then a smile spread over the journalist's features.

"What an idiot I am! After all, there's no danger ...it was a happy thought of mine leaving that note for Juve ...he'll come to-morrow at the latest ...that gives me the rest of the night."

Fandor's ruse, its daring and its almost unheard of devotion, appeared to him quite natural. It was simply to set the King at liberty and remain himself in his place.

While he undoubtedly ran the risk of a bullet in his body, yet the carefully drawn plan he had left in Juve's rooms would enable the detective to find his prison without difficulty.

The first problem that presented itself was to get the drunken King away.

Frederick-Christian lay, an inert mass, quite incapable of rendering any assistance. Fandor began by drawing himself up to the opening and taking a look around. The Place de la Concorde was deserted.

"Well, to work!" he cried. "There is nothing for me to do but to haul him out, then put the body of the statue back in place....If in three days nothing happens, why I shall be free to leave. The ham will keep me going, and as for the wine ...Ah! an idea!"

The journalist seized half a dozen of the empty bottles, climbed out and filled them with water; returning, he drew from his pocket a thin silk cord he had taken from Juve's room. By its aid and with a strength of which his slender figure gave no evidence, he succeeded in hauling the King up to the open air.

"And now for another foot bath," exclaimed Fandor; "saving Kings is a sorry business."

Having waded again through the icy water of the basin, Fandor carried the unconscious monarch upon his shoulders and deposited his burden on the sidewalk. He was about to regain his dungeon when he suddenly paused:

"The deuce! I was forgetting! When he becomes sober again, he'll have forgotten all about his adventure ...he'll kick up a row at the Royal Palace....I must warn him."

Fandor took out his notebook, wrote a few lines which he enclosed in an envelope and pinned it upon the King's coat. Upon the envelope was written:

"I am to read this when I wake."

His next proceeding was to blow a shrill whistle.

"It's your turn now, my dear Wulf ...you won't find the fair unknown you expect, but you'll get back your Prince, slightly the worse for wear."

The journalist now swung the statue back in place, exclaiming:

"Au revoir, Monsieur, I'm off to take your place ...sorry I can't stay to see the meeting with Wulf ...he'll find his King somewhat changed....I ought to have given you my moustache and beard."

Fandor passed a horrible night. He was obliged to economize the use of his electric lamp, which was only capable of giving several hours of light, so after a careful survey of his lodging, he extinguished it and lay down to get what rest he could.

"Not much fun for the King here!" he thought, "it's devilish monotonous ...can't see anything, and nothing to hear ...hold on, I can distinguish three separate noises, the plash of the water from the fountains, the rumble of carriages, and that heavy sound can only be the passage of trains from the North-South in the tunnel, which if I mistake not is right under my prison ...and these Singing Fountains ...they are accounted for by the King howling when he got drunk ...but what about the night Susy d'Orsel was killed?...The King wasn't here then, and yet they were heard singing?"

Fandor was not long in reaching the solution of the mystery.

"What a fool I am!...the murder of Susy d'Orsel, the imprisonment of the King, are both the work of Fantômas! Fantômas must have known this hiding place a long time ago....It was he who tried the experiment of making the statues sing to find out whether the sound could be heard above....And to think that this monster has been arrested by Juve! And without me, too!...I shall have only the glory of showing up a few of his accomplices, and if they don't come in two or three days, why, I shall clear out."

Fandor rose and went toward the base of the naiad.

"It's still dark. I might just as well get a breath of fresh air."

With a gymnastic leap, the journalist reached the body of the statue and switched on his electric light. He made a horrible discovery. To reach the King he had maneuvered the statue from the outside. He realized now that it was impossible to open it from the inside. In his daring folly he had shut himself in and possibly condemned himself to the most terrible torture.

Now he began a struggle to regain his liberty. He tore his fingers and broke his nails in vain despairing efforts ...at length he gave up, beaten. He was irrevocably a prisoner. When he realized his situation he sank to the ground, a cry escaping his lips:

"Juve! Juve! If only Juve finds my letter. If only he comes to save me!"

CHAPTER XX
FREDERICK-CHRISTIAN

"Another drink, Monsieur Louis?"

"I think I've had about enough."

"No, no ... this is my turn to treat."

"Well, since you put it that way, Monsieur Wulf, I can't refuse."

"Besides," added the barkeeper, "this is some very special vermouth, only served to old clients."

"Ah," laughed Wulf, "I hope we're included in that category, for you certainly have no better client than myself."

"Excuse me," replied the barkeeper, smiling, "we have one, your boss, Monsieur Wulf, the King Frederick-Christian.... And while he doesn't always finish his drinks he always pays for them."

"And that's the important thing," added M. Louis.

It was about ten in the morning, and in the bar of the Royal Palace, deserted at this early hour, were M. Louis, Major-domo of the hotel, Wulf, and the barkeeper, who in his turn offered a round of drinks on the house.

As the glasses were being filled, the telephone rang to say that his Majesty wanted to see Wulf.

"That's all right," replied Wulf condescendingly, "I'll be along by and by."

After several more vermouths, Wulf grew expansive:

"Do you know, Monsieur Louis, that I've actually saved the King's life twice in five days!"

"Pretty good work," commented M. Louis, politely.

"The first time was the day after my arrival in Paris. Your Government wanted to kick up a fuss over the death of the King's little sweetheart; in fact, they went so far as to talk of his arrest." Wulf stopped suddenly, alarmed:

"But that is a state secret which I may not tell you. The second time was yesterday evening, or rather early this morning. You see the King and I had been off on a spree together."

As the barkeeper looked surprised at this announcement, Wulf explained:

"Oh, we're a couple of pals, the King and I ... like two fingers of one hand ... that's why I was in no hurry to answer his call just now.... Well, as I was saying, we were having a little spree, and the King was going to introduce me to a little ... but that's another secret.... I'll skip the details, it is enough to say that after waiting a while, I found, instead of the girl, the King, my King. And where? Beside the Singing Fountains in the Place de la Concorde. Ah! my dear friends, what a state he was in! I hardly knew him at first; in fact, I shouldn't have known him at all if I were not such a sharp detective. He had removed his false beard and spectacles. I tell you Frederick-Christian has aged ten years, his clothes were torn and covered with mud, and moreover he was dead drunk! How he managed it in the time I don't know, for he wasn't away from me for more than an hour. What would you have done in my place? Left there in that deserted street he would have been at the mercy of the first thief or assassin. Therefore, I say, I saved his life by putting him into a cab and bringing him back to the Royal Palace. While I was helping to put him to bed, I noticed a letter pinned to his coat with this inscription on it, 'I am to read this when I wake.' So I have arranged accordingly. He'll see it the first thing on opening his eyes. Well, what do you think of that? Didn't I save the King's life a second time?"

M. Louis nodded:

"Never twice without the third time."

"I hope so ... well, au revoir, Monsieur...."

"Pardon, Monsieur," interrupted one of the employés, "but his Majesty has asked for you again."

"All right, I'm going," replied Wulf, as he drank his fifth vermouth.

"Whatever happens, whatever you are told, do not show any surprise. Take up your customary life again as though it had never been interrupted, as though nothing had happened since the night of December 31st."

Frederick-Christian, the victim of a racking headache, read and reread these strange mysterious words, without in the least understanding their meaning. After a heavy sleep, he had wakened about nine o'clock to find himself lying comfortably in his own bed at the Royal Palace. At first he thought it was part of his nightmare, that he was dreaming, but as he became more fully awake, he was obliged to admit the evidence of his senses.

At this moment, he suddenly caught sight of the crumpled letter pinned to his counterpane; opening it, he read the lines that Fandor had hurriedly pencilled the night before.

In spite of his exhaustion and stiffness, he sprang out of bed and was about to ring for a servant when a feeling of caution came over him.

It would be better first to take stock of the situation.

What had happened?

Among the newspapers lying on the table, he noticed several copies of the *Gazette* of Hesse-Weimar.

He glanced over the most recent numbers, but found nothing unusual in their columns. He then went back to the paper dated January 1st and to his amazement saw the following announcement:

"Paris, 1st January. (From our Special Correspondent.) His Majesty Frederick-Christian, contrary to his general custom, did not leave his Hotel during New Year's Day. This may be accounted for by the fact that the streets of Paris are, as a rule, crowded during this holiday and his Majesty would have run the risk of being drawn into promiscuous contact with the common people."

The copy of January 2d also remarked that the King had evinced a desire to attend the Longchamps races, but had been prevented by the possibility of a chance meeting with the President of the Republic, a contingency not foreseen in the protocol. Frederick-Christian, in fact, recalled that he had expressed a wish to attend the Longchamps meet, but he asked himself how it was possible to have notified him of the change of program while at that time he had mysteriously disappeared! But the climax of his amazement was reached when he came to the following paragraph:

"Paris, 4th January. (From our Special Correspondent.) His Majesty Frederick-Christian II is still held in the French Capital by affairs of the highest importance. His subjects need, however, be under no apprehension, as his Majesty's health is excellent, this information having been received by Hedwige, our well-beloved Queen.

"During his stay in Paris, Frederick-Christian has been especially appreciative of the respectful and devoted services of M. Wulfenmimenglaschk, head of the secret service of Hesse-Weimar, who, by the exercise of his perspicacity and high intelligence, has found in the King not only an able assistant, but a true friend, having the honor to occupy the apartment at the Royal Palace next to his Majesty."

"What's this all about?" exclaimed the King, "what influence have I been under during these last four days?"

It was easy enough to recommend him to show no surprise, but it was also necessary to settle upon some definite attitude to take. And what about this "Wulf"?

Frederick-Christian would have a look at this individual who claimed to be his friend and his next door neighbor. Accordingly he rang the bell, and sent down the message which Wulf received in the barroom. A wait of twenty minutes followed and then the door opened without ceremony and the King stood rooted in amazement at the appearance of his Secret Service Chief. In the most natural manner in the world, Wulf entered the room and stood looking slyly at the King. Then, smilingly, he said:

"Well, Sire, feel better?"

"What!" stuttered Frederick-Christian, scarcely able to speak for indignation.

"Yes," continued Wulf, "I'm glad to see you up; as for me, I'm all right ... but you must remember that I drank less than you did last night. I tell you they've capital vermouth here ... shall I order your Majesty a bottle?"

"What's your name?" asked the King.

Wulf considered his sovereign with compassion.

"He's still a bit soused," he muttered to himself, then wagging a reproving finger at the King, he continued:

"Who am I? Wulfenmimenglaschk, Sire, at your service, and I've already saved your life twice ... that's why I may be allowed to give you a bit of advice. Cut out the booze, Sire, you're distinctly the worse for wear ... you're so changed that if it wasn't for your dressing-gown...."

Wulf was undoubtedly very drunk; otherwise he could not have failed to notice the difference between the King of the last few days and the present one.

Frederick-Christian held himself in hand as long as possible, then burst out:

"What does this attitude mean?... this familiarity? What makes you speak in French?"

Wulf was first amazed at the change in his beloved master and inclined to weep over his humiliation. He was about to give utterance to his feelings when the King seized him by the arm and pointed to the *Hesse-Weimar Gazette*.

"Read that! Who furnished this information?"

"Why, I did, Sire."

"Then you mean to say you have been continually with me. You occupy the next apartment? You enjoy my friendship?"

"Yes, Sire."

The King, in a burst of rage, now held the unfortunate Wulf by the collar and shoving him toward the door, ejected him onto the landing with a prodigious kick.

Frederick-Christian, more puzzled than ever by the turn of events, now turned his attention to his toilette. He was still in scanty attire and went behind his screen to continue dressing. At this moment a soft and charming voice spoke:

"Sire, are you there? It is I ... Marie Pascal."

Marie Pascal!

Where had he heard that name before? Slowly Frederick-Christian recalled the silhouette of a young woman ... with a fair skin and light hair...

The voice continued:

"I am glad to know that you are better, Sire. Forgive me for troubling you now but since our last meeting things have happened of a very serious nature ... hidden enemies want to destroy me ... to destroy us.... First of all they accused your Majesty of the murder of Susy d'Orsel, and now after torturing me with questions they have dared to say it was I!... I'm sure they overheard our last conversation and misunderstand our love for each other...."

Frederick-Christian was growing suspicious. What did this extraordinary visit mean? Did they want to trap him into an unwary admission?

"In the name of our love, say you don't believe me guilty!"

The King hesitated.

"I don't know.... I ..."

He stopped short as Marie Pascal with a sudden movement flung down the screen. The King in amaze stood stock still while the young girl looked at him in utter stupefaction, with trembling lips and body shaken by nervous tremors. Then suddenly she turned in terror, screaming:

"Help! Help! The impostor! The murderer!... the King is not the King.... Frederick-Christian has disappeared!... Who is this man?"

The girl's cries brought the Hotel servants quickly to the scene. She continued, pointing to the King:

"Who is this man?... Frederick-Christian has disappeared!... good God, what has happened?"

"Better call the police," suggested some one.

This met with general approval, but proceedings were suddenly interrupted by the arrival of Wulf.

"Have you heard?" several voices asked.

"All I know," replied Wulf in a piteous tone, "is that Frederick-Christian or not, he's got a devilish heavy foot, and when he kicks, he kicks royally."

CHAPTER XXI
HORRIBLE CERTAINTY

"What has happened to that idiot Juve? Here for three days I've been shut up in this beastly prison and no sign of him."

As the days passed, Fandor gradually lost his buoyancy of spirits and became more and more anxious.

"What can Juve be doing?" he repeated for the hundredth time.

The continual obscurity of the place began to weigh him down. This was relieved each day for a few moments by a thin shaft of light. Fandor was quick to account for the phenomenon.

"It happens exactly at noon when the sun is directly overhead," he reasoned, "and finds an entrance through a crack in the bronze."

Many times he climbed to the body of the naiad in the hope of discovering some method of escape, but at length he realized that the thing was impossible.

He was seated one night deep in thought, puzzling his brains for the reason of Juve's defection, when a voice suddenly broke the silence.

"Can you hear me?"

Fandor bounded to his feet.

"Yes, I hear you."

"You must be getting uneasy?"

"Uneasy! I'm going mad! What a long time you've been!"

"That's true, I am a little late, but it hasn't been very easy."

Now that Fandor's mind was set at rest about his deliverance, he grew curious to know the results of the detective's investigation.

"Well, you were successful?"

"Yes, quite successful."

"Do they know in Glotzbourg?"

"They must have some suspicion by now."

"When did you get back?"

"This morning."

"Only this morning! And did you get my letter?"

"Your what, Sire?...I don't catch."

"I say you must have got my letter, since you are here, and now please get me out of this hole as quickly as possible ...it's awful being shut up here ...you can't imagine how I long for a breath of fresh air."

"Yes, yes, I understand, but I'm wondering how I'm to get you out."

"What's that?"

"Have you thought over a way we can effect the exchange?"

"But, my dear fellow, you must know what to do. I gave you full particulars in my letter."

"In your letter?"

"Yes....I even enclosed a diagram."

There was a pause, the voice then asked:

"Will you pass me up this letter by..."

Fandor interrupted:

"Why, it's quite simple! Find the third naiad, counting from the one nearest the bridge."

Suddenly the voice explained:

"Look here, Sire, we are talking at cross purposes. I am asking you where we can exchange the diamond."

"The diamond?"

"Yes! Your diamond."

Fandor's face grew pale.

"My diamond!"

"The diamond I went to Glotzbourg to get ... what's the matter with you, Sire? Don't you remember?... And what's all this about a letter?"

"Why, Juve! I'm talking of the letter I left at your apartment in which I explained how you may reach me!"

"Juve! Juve! Oho!"

A burst of strident laughter, infernal and diabolical, reached Fandor, who now guessed the horrible truth.

"If it isn't Juve who is speaking, who is it?" he cried. "For the love of God, who are you?"

"The person speaking to you ... is Fantômas."

"Fantômas!"

Staggering, terrified, Fandor screamed:

"Fantômas! Fantômas!... It can't be possible! Fantômas has been arrested! Fantômas is in the hands of Juve!"

"Fantômas arrested?... Fantômas can't be arrested! He will never be caught! He is above and beyond every attack, every menace! Fantômas is Death, Eternal Death, Pitiless Death, King Death! Good-bye!"

A long silence followed. Fandor was stunned by the awful reality. He experienced all the sensations of a man buried alive, condemned to death with torture. And then another thought flashed through his mind:

"The papers spoke of Fantômas's arrest. But if Fantômas is at liberty, it must mean that Juve has been beaten! Juve went to Glotzbourg to arrest him. A man has been arrested under the name of Fantômas. That man must be Juve himself!"

And his letter! The first thing Fantômas would do would be to go to Juve's apartment and destroy it.

"He has got me," he exclaimed. "He can choose his own time to kill me. He can send down asphyxiating gas or a deluge of water through the connecting tube, or he can just leave me here to die slowly of hunger and thirst."

The journalist began pacing up and down his prison. He tried to recover his calm and argue the case out:

"Here I am in perfect health, clear in my mind and able to struggle to the bitter end. I have enough food and water to last me about nine or ten days. In my pocket I have my revolver, so that I can blow my brains out if it comes to the worst. But I won't. I'll fight! I'll fight until I drop!"

CHAPTER XXII
BETWEEN US THREE — FANTÔMAS!

For the second time, the Grand Duchess Alexandra solemnly repeated to the Queen:

"I have the honor to take leave of your Majesty, and I dare to hope that I may hear news of your Majesty when I reach my journey's end. I shall be away a long while from the court of Hesse-Weimar and from its august Sovereign for whom I profess the deepest respect."

The interview between the Queen and the woman she deemed her mortal enemy took place about eleven o'clock, two days after the famous ball in the midst of which the detective Juve had so unfortunately been mistaken for Fantômas, and thrown into a gloomy dungeon where he had since been kept in solitary confinement. Opinion at Hesse-Weimar was divided between the theory that the thief had succeeded in hiding the famous diamond before he was caught, and the theory that when he discovered its hiding place, he had found an empty jewel case.

Naturally, the identity of the Grand Duchess with the famous Lady Beltham,[3] established by Juve, was unknown in Hesse-Weimar, nor did anyone suspect that her sudden departure was in any way connected with the arrest of the pseudo Fantômas.

The Queen was at first unwilling to believe in the retreat of her enemy, but she was at length obliged to accept the fact when Alexandra made her formal adieux.

"There was a rumor that you were going to leave us," she replied, "but I scarcely credited it, Madame."

The adventuress, who by a series of extraordinary circumstances had been enabled to pass herself as a cousin of the reigning family, looked at the Queen sadly:

"Your Majesty is not very kind to me," she exclaimed with tears in her voice, "and I hoped for a more friendly farewell at the moment when I am taking my departure for the new world."

The Queen was touched by these words; with an impulsive movement she opened her arms to the false Grand Duchess, who flung herself into them in a long embrace.

The two women now had a heart to heart talk in which the Queen confessed her fears and distrust. She even went to the length of admitting her belief that Alexandra had had designs upon the throne of Hesse-Weimar.

The adventuress looked with pitying contempt upon the little Queen Hedwige:

"Your Majesty has been outrageously deceived," she replied, "I belong to a race which is incapable of such treachery."

Completely reassured, the Queen became very tender and ended affectionately by wishing the pseudo Duchess a good journey. The two women parted friends.

On a siding in the Glotzbourg station stood a private car, which had been placed at the service of the Grand Duchess, waiting to be connected with the Paris express from Berlin.

Inside, the Duchess, dressed in a quiet traveling costume, sat talking to Prince Gudulfin. The young man was pale and anxious:

"Your orders have been carried out, Madame, are you satisfied?"

The pseudo Grand Duchess thanked the Prince with a softened look, and the latter continued in a low voice:

"Madame, you know that my followers are prepared to try a *coup d'état* — for pity's sake accept the homage of my love, give me a word of hope, and I will overthrow the present dynasty and mount the throne myself with you as my Queen."

"That is nothing but a mad dream, Prince … something impossible to happen … we have not the right even to think of it."

"You are more than unkind to me, Madame … you are enigmatic … mysterious."

At this moment a newsboy was heard crying an extra edition of the *Hesse-Weimar Gazette*. The Duchess rose quickly and bought a copy.

In large headlines she read the following:

"Death of Fantômas. The bandit ends his days in prison."

Alexandra sat down and became absorbed in the details, paying no further attention to Prince Gudulfin.

At length after a long pause, he spoke bitterly:

"This bandit seems to interest you more than I do, Madame."

The Grand Duchess made a vague gesture of denial.

The Prince sighed:

"Ah, you might remember that in this sinister business, the account of which you are now reading, it is owing to me your wishes have been carried out. You have been obeyed blindly."

Lady Beltham was spared the necessity of replying, for at this moment the express entered the station with a deafening roar. As it was scheduled to remain only a few minutes, the private car was hurriedly attached to the end of the train. In the ensuing hurry and scurry of passengers who were anxiously being scrutinized by the Grand Duchess, there appeared a man dressed in dark clothes, and wearing a gray beard. He was searching hurriedly through the cars for an empty seat. The Duchess gave a faint cry at the sight of him, and withdrew to the back of her compartment.

Who was it?

The train whistled and the last good-byes were said.

Prince Gudulfin pleaded so urgently for a tender word, that the adventuress, with the consummate art of the actress, leaned out, whispering:

"Hope, Prince, hope ... some day, perhaps ... later ... and remember that even the most virtuous of women, when she cannot give encouragement, is not averse to leaving regrets behind her."

During the evening which preceded Lady Beltham's departure, Juve sat in his cell eating his frugal repast.

For forty-eight hours he had seen no one except his two jailors, and he was beginning to worry over his situation. There had now been plenty of time for them to discover their mistake in arresting him. His eyes had pained him greatly the first day but were now slowly recovering. Feeling a desire to sleep, Juve stretched himself on his bed and gave way to reflection.

What had happened?

It was not difficult to guess. The officers of the Palace, finding him in the King's bedroom, a smoking revolver beside him and a Lancer crying "Thief! thief!" had naturally arrested him, thinking him guilty. Fantômas, after blinding him with pepper, had changed back into his uniform and escaped with the diamond. But what was Lady Beltham doing there known to the Hesse-Weimar people as the Grand Duchess Alexandra? What new and diabolical projects were on foot to bring the monster and his mistress together in this honest, bourgeois court of Hesse-Weimar?

As for the diamond, of what possible use could it be to the thief? It would be harder to get rid of than the obelisk or the Vendôme column!

While these thoughts were passing slowly through Juve's mind, he felt an intense desire to sleep come over him, his limbs suddenly became numb and heavy; and then a sudden terror seized him.

"I have been poisoned!" he cried, making a superhuman effort to rise; but the narcotic was slowly but surely overpowering him. Finally, he lost all idea of his surroundings and sank back on his bed unconscious.

Had the day come?

A pale light touched with yellow and silver rays, crept softly through the half-opened door and reached the face of a sleeping man; causing him to stir and to open his eyes, blinking and yawning. It was Juve.

The first thing his gaze lighted upon was a round moon in a blue sky sown with stars. The detective who had gone to sleep in a dungeon, smiled instinctively at the heavens and the fresh, pure air which filled the room. By degrees his mind went back to the events of the past night, the heavy sleep that had come over him, and he wondered how much time had elapsed since he had lost consciousness. He had, besides, the impression that beneath his ample and warm bed clothes he was quite naked. His movements, too, seemed constricted as though he were lying in a narrow frame bed placed on the ground.

But where was he?

Thanks to the moonlight, he could perceive that he was in a room on the ground floor. Outside, shapes flitted by, and these Juve soon found to be bats hurrying to their nearby lairs. An owl hooted in the distance. The detective determined to make an effort to get up. To his surprise he met with no resistance and easily climbed out of the sort of box in which he had been lying.

As his eyes became accustomed to the semi-obscurity, he started upon seeing the bed he had been lying in. It was a coffin.

Juve then shuddered at the thought of the horrible death he might have undergone. He might have been buried alive! But a further surprise was in store for him. Not far away stood another coffin, and in this second one lay a corpse.

The dead man was about fifty, strongly built and robust. A small clot of blood had congealed on his temple and this was enough to show Juve the cause of his death.

He had been shot through the head with a revolver, and his death had been instantaneous. The rigidity of the body showed that the crime had been committed some time before. And then he made a still further discovery. By the side of the coffin lay a pile of clothes, and to Juve's amazement he recognized them as being his own!

"Well," he exclaimed, "there can be no harm in putting them on, since they are mine." A further search disclosed, tucked away in a corner of the coffin, his pocketbook. Not only that, but some generous person had stuffed it literally full of bank notes, and in a small pocket he also found a first-class ticket from Glotzbourg to the frontier.

"What on earth does all this mean?" he exclaimed.

A search of his erstwhile bed now brought to light a sheet torn from a railway time-table, upon which a certain train was underscored in red ink. From another corner of the coffin he brought out a false beard and a pair of yellow spectacles! In a twinkling Juve dressed himself and crossing to the door, pushed it open and looked out.

"The deuce!" he cried, "that's a funereal outlook!"

Before him stretched away on all sides ... tombstones! tombstones big and little — some with crosses, others with crowns and flowers.

Juve was in a cemetery, and the strange room in which he found himself was the mortuary chapel. Nothing disturbed the impressive silence of this vast resting place. In the distance a clock struck five, and far off Juve perceived the silhouette of the Glotzbourg Cathedral.

The detective pulled himself together and began to piece out by his well-known habit of induction some solution to this incomprehensible mystery.

"To begin with," he exclaimed, "my being still alive is evidently due to the will of my adversaries. It is possible that the police of Hesse-Weimar may have discovered their mistake, and taken this method of setting me at liberty. Or, it has been given out that I am dead, and they intend to bury this poor fellow in my place....

"No, that's stupid. I was forgetting it is Fantômas who is supposed to be caught, then are they going to give out that Fantômas is dead?...That seems out of the question....Besides this man didn't die a natural death, he was killed! I can't make head or tail of it."

Juve paced up and down, rejecting one hypothesis after another. Finally, with a shrug of his shoulders, he cried:

"Bah! I shall know all in good time. Let's get to the most pressing problem. I have been given money, a ticket with the time of departure marked on the time-table, that is as much as to say:

"'My dear Sir, you are to go to the Station and take the 1.22 train, first class, for the frontier, there you will be left to your own devices ... but be careful to use the disguise given you.'"

"Well," continued Juve to himself, "I haven't the least desire to thwart my mysterious friends, having no wish to prolong my visit here."

Soon afterward Juve set out toward the town. As he walked the dawn broke on the horizon.

For three hours the Berlin express had been speeding across Hesse-Weimar on its way to Paris. Night was beginning to fall and multi-colored signals showed their points of light as the train sped past way stations.

Juve, plunged in his thoughts, paid no attention to what was passing without. He had picked up a copy of the *Hesse-Weimar Gazette* before leaving, and in it had read the following:

"The desperate bandit, Fantômas, arrested two days ago in the Royal Palace while in the act of stealing the diamond, has committed suicide by shooting himself through the head with a small revolver he had hidden in his clothes. His body is now lying in the mortuary chapel of the cemetery awaiting the inevitable autopsy."

This information but confirmed Juve in the hypothesis he had formed. But there still remained a point to be cleared up. Undoubtedly the public were being duped ... but who was duping them, and why? If Juve was thought to be Fantômas, they wouldn't have let him escape and put a dead man in his place. On the other hand, if they knew that Juve was not Fantômas, why the devil had this suicide story been invented?

A new idea suddenly flashed through Juve's mind.

"Suppose that not only the people of Hesse-Weimar but also the Government have been fooled!"

A glimpse caught of Prince Gudulfin descending from the private car at the Hesse-Weimar station, was sufficient to start this train of thought. By association of ideas the sight of the Prince brought to Juve's mind the figure of the Grand Duchess Alexandra, who was no other than Lady Beltham. And Lady Beltham suggested Fantômas, whom Juve was inclined to credit not only with his arrest but also with his liberation.

When the train pulled into the Frontier Station Juve, still wearing his false beard and whiskers, jumped down and hurried to the ticket office to buy his transportation to Paris. As he was returning, he happened to glance at the private car attached to the train at Glotzbourg, when, in spite of his self-control, he could not repress a cry of triumph.

One of the window curtains was suddenly raised and then immediately lowered again, but Juve had time to recognize a face. It was that of the Grand Duchess Alexandra ... otherwise Lady Beltham. The train whistled.

Juve had only just time to regain his compartment. He began pacing up and down the corridor, rubbing his hands, almost jumping for joy. At last the mystery was cleared. He understood what had been going on. Lady Beltham had fainted when Juve was arrested. Why?

Evidently, because she had accepted the general opinion that he was Fantômas. After coming to herself and learning that the monster was in prison, she had made up her mind to effect his escape cost what it might.

But how was she to set about it?

Doubtless Lady Beltham, in her capacity of Grand Duchess, had many devoted friends, and it was evidently with their aid that the evasion had been brought about. And Lady Beltham, herself a dupe, still imagined it was her lover she had saved; when in reality she had set at liberty his most determined enemy.

As the air now began to grow chilly, Juve returned to his compartment and picked up his overcoat. He was about to put it on, when he stopped in amazement.

On the lining was pinned a paper with the following words scribbled in pencil:

"America Hotel, Paris."

For a long time Juve, with bent brows, read and reread these words. They could only have been brought here by Lady Beltham herself while Juve was away getting his ticket. What did this mysterious address portend?

If Lady Beltham believed she was communicating with Fantômas, she certainly would have no need to write to him; she would know well enough where to find him.

Furthermore, why didn't she simply walk through the several intervening cars and talk to him? What could be the motive powerful enough to prevent the mistress rejoining her lover?

Upon second thoughts Juve doubted the hypothesis that Lady Beltham had intended to instigate the release of Fantômas. Might she not have become weary of the yoke which joined her to this monster and be really repentant of her crimes? It would not be the first time she had tasted remorse — and, instead of saving Fantômas, was aware that Juve had been set at liberty.

"Yes," echoed Juve, "this second hypothesis is evidently the right one and Lady Beltham has ranged herself upon the side of law."

The detective, with a defiant glance at the deepening evening shadows, proclaimed grandiloquently:

"So be it, Lady Beltham, it shall not be said that a gallant man repays you with ingratitude, and if you care to have it so we will say in unison:

"Between us three, Fantômas!"

The train thundered through the night. It was only at seven in the morning that the suburbs of Paris showed through an uncertain fog.

Saint Denis, the fortifications, and then the train slowed up and stopped under the great glass dome of the Gare du Nord. Juve, waking with a start, hastily sprang out and made his way to the private car in the hope of seeing Lady Beltham. But the Lady had already disappeared.... Juve caught up with her just in time to see her enter an automobile which instantly got under way. He managed to catch the number of the car, but could not find a taxi rapid enough to make the attempt of overtaking her.

"Oh, well," he exclaimed, "I know how to find her."

A sudden thought struck him:

"The delay accorded me by M. Annion expires to-day, and the arrest of the false Frederick-Christian is about due. I don't suppose Fandor has taken any steps, but I'd better find out what is happening."

Juve consulted his watch:

"Half-past seven, I can call on the Minister of the Interior."

He sprang into a taxi and cried:

"Number eleven, Rue des Saussaies!"

CHAPTER XXIII
OFFICIAL OPINIONS

"Well, M. Vicart?"

"Well, M. Annion, that's all."

"That's all!" replied M. Annion. "That's nothing! We've been talking for a quarter of an hour without getting anywhere or reaching any conclusion."

"But, M. Annion...."

"No, I say....It is I who have been giving you all the information and that, you know, is rather surprising....You are the acting head of the Secret Service and you should have known all this. It's not my place to tell you what's going on at the Royal Palace."

"M. Annion, nothing at all has happened."

This reply threw M. Annion into a sudden fit of anger.

"Is that so? Nothing has happened, hasn't it? And you don't realize the gravity of the case! Really, Vicart, it's discouraging! Can't you understand that we must absolutely come to some decision? The ministry is under the constant threat of interpellations and that state of affairs cannot continue."

"Oh, I don't say the situation isn't serious, I only say nothing new has turned up."

"That's just what I'm complaining about — your absolute lack of comprehension. To begin with, a week has gone by ...a whole week since Juve left, and not a word from Glotzbourg.... In fact, Juve is a day late already....Does that convey nothing to you?...To me it means that Juve has found nothing there."

"I don't quite understand," ventured the bewildered Vicart.

M. Annion took pity on his subordinate.

"Before Juve left he had proved to me that the King was the real King; isn't that so?"

"Yes."

"But that doesn't alter the fact that the King is a murderer....Juve suspected some court intrigue, that's why he left for Glotzbourg. Now what is our situation? We have a King who has committed murder, and we don't arrest him. But that is the least of my worries. What about public opinion on the one hand and the extraordinary audacity of this monarch on the other?"

"Public opinion?"

"Yes! why the deuce don't you read the papers? Learn what is going on! Take the opposition press — they're always hinting at the weakness of the government in not arresting criminals on account of diplomatic complications. While I've seen to it that no more manifestations take place outside the Royal Palace, that the public for the time being is muzzled, still it is only waiting a chance to break out again. And now here is Frederick-Christian writing to the Minister of Foreign Affairs saying he wishes to meet the President of the Republic ...while he is here incognito. Still, by the terms of the protocol, he owes a visit to the Elysée — he's right about that."

"Well, what then?"

"Why, it complicates things very awkwardly. How can the President receive, especially incognito, a King who is thought to be an assassin ...you don't know what might be made of it.... This extraordinary Frederick-Christian takes advantage of his impunity. He's had lots of time since the death of Susy to slip quietly back to his own country....That would have let us out ... instead of which he comes out in the limelight ...gets himself talked about ...a nice time to choose, I must say!"

M. Annion was interrupted by the entrance of a clerk who handed him a visiting card.

"Who is it now?...Ah ...show them in."

He then turned to M. Vicart:

"Don't go....It may be something connected with the King."

The door was opened and the visitors announced:

"M. the Commissaire of Police Giraud — Mlle. Marie Pascal."

"Well, Monsieur Giraud ... take a seat, Mademoiselle ... what have you come about?"

"A very serious business," answered M. Giraud. "I have come to see you after a visit from Mlle. Marie Pascal. She will repeat to you the extraordinary things she has said to me."

"What is it all about, Mademoiselle?"

Pale and anxious, Marie Pascal rose and advanced to M. Annion's desk, and said, with a trembling voice:

"Monsieur, I went to M. Giraud about a call I wanted to make on his Majesty Frederick-Christian, King of Hesse-Weimar."

"Yes?"

"Well, Monsieur, I was not received by the King."

M. Annion evinced no surprise.

"Unless I am mistaken you are the lace-maker who was so tragically mixed up in the death of Susy d'Orsel?... It was you who found the chemise ... it was you who ... however, go ahead, Mademoiselle, you were received by a secretary, by a chamberlain?"

"No! no! I was received by the King, but by a King who wasn't the real one, but an impostor!"

"Good God!" cried M. Annion.

Here was this impostor affair cropping up again. The girl must be crazy.

"But it's unbelievable! Come, Mademoiselle, weigh well the gravity of your words — you can scarcely be making this up as a joke, I hope. You can furnish absolute proof of what you say? Why do you think the King is not the King?"

Marie Pascal had recovered her self-control, and she gave M. Annion a detailed account of the audience she had obtained with Frederick-Christian. She hid nothing, neither his former warmth of feeling nor his recent coldness. She explained that his face no longer looked the same, nor had his voice the same sound, that he had attempted to hide behind the screen and finally that she was quite sure the man she saw was not the King.

"What did you do, Mademoiselle?"

This time M. Giraud spoke up:

"Mlle. Marie was wrong in what she did, but under the stress of emotion she raised the whole hotel and made such a row that M. Louis advised her to come and see me."

"Very good, and then?"

"Why, M. Annion, I hurried to the Royal Palace and made an investigation, where I confirmed what Mademoiselle had told me. I then decided I had better lay the matter before you."

M. Annion sat deep in thought for a few moments. Then he burst out:

"Hang it! Your accusation of imposture is absurd, Mademoiselle, utterly impossible!" Then, turning to M. Vicart, he added:

"Haven't we the formal declaration, irrefutable, of that Secret Service man ... Glaschk..."

"Wulfenmimenglaschk."

"That's it!... Have you seen him, M. Giraud?"

"I have, but I couldn't get anything out of him; he was three-quarters drunk, and furious with his Majesty who had just struck him."

M. Annion stared in amazement.

"But Frederick-Christian was his friend — his intimate friend ... they were pals ... and you say he struck him?"

Crossing quickly to the telephone, he called up:

"Hello! Are inspectors 42, 59 and 63 there? What? Then send them up."

"You did well to come to me, M. Giraud; we must clear up this business at any cost.... I've just sent for the three inspectors whom I detailed this morning to watch his Majesty Frederick-Christian...."

Then glancing at Marie Pascal:

"You'll hear what they have to say, Mademoiselle." A few minutes later the three men entered the office.

"Well, what is new? You've been shadowing him?"

"Yes, Monsieur."

"Anything to report?"

"Nothing much, Monsieur, only in regard to the conduct of the King. It seems that since this morning he has quite changed. Frederick-Christian, instead of keeping himself shut up as of late, now sees his friends again and has resumed his haughty manner and his fault-finding with the servants."

"What friends has he seen?"

"A young attaché of the Embassy arrived immediately after luncheon, and the director of his bank."

"And these men found nothing unusual?"

"No, chief, nothing at all."

M. Annion turned to Marie Pascal.

"You see, Mademoiselle, that is conclusive, isn't it? What probably happened was that the King had a fit of nerves, due to the death of his mistress, and then his return to his normal life misled you...."

Marie Pascal interrupted:

"No, Monsieur, no! Your inspectors are wrong! I who love him cannot be deceived! It is no longer Frederick-Christian II who is at the Royal Palace, it is an impostor! Besides, even if I could have been mistaken, he had no reason for not recognizing me, of not seeming to understand what I was saying."

The second inspector spoke up:

"Chief, I have something which will convince Mademoiselle that she is mistaken. I was able to get hold of one of his Majesty's collars which he had just worn. Its size is distinctly characteristic, being 18 inches. Now it would be very easy to verify the fact that the real King wears this size and also whether it fits the supposed impostor. In any case, Monsieur, from inquiries made among the hotel servants I find there can be no doubt that Frederick-Christian is actually staying there, and that his intimate friends have been received and have recognized him."

M. Annion did not answer.

"This Marie Pascal is crazy," he thought, "or else she is up to some game which I don't understand... the King is the King all right, but, hang it all, that doesn't alter the fact that he is an assassin."

CHAPTER XXIV
JUVE'S LIES

M. Annion had left the Ministry quite late the evening before in a very bad humor. Not that he had any doubt about the deposition of Marie Pascal. The report of his inspectors had settled that point, supplemented by the visits to the King of the attaché and the banker.

"That young girl of the sixth floor," he said to himself, "who calls herself Marie Pascal, is either trying to hold up the sovereign or else she is crazy. In either case the important thing is to make her hold her tongue. Now there are two ways of doing this, through menacing her or through bribing her. I'll apply the first, and if that doesn't answer I'll try the second."

As to the King, while his identity had been proved, he was none the less a murderer.

The question was whether to prevent the visit he wished to pay to the President of the Republic or to bring it about.

M. Annion took the Rue des Saussaies at 7.30 and having reached home, dined quickly while he read the evening paper. The news was startling.

An article reserved in tone, but giving sufficient details, announced the arrest of Fantômas, the mysterious criminal of the Palace Royal of Glotzbourg, while attempting to steal the diamond which constituted the private fortune of Prince Frederick-Christian II.

"Good God!" cried M. Annion, "Fantômas arrested, the diamond stolen, and Juve doesn't return or send any word!"

The director of the Secret Service felt himself entangled in a network of intrigues which seemed impossible to unravel. He seemed to be surrounded by an impenetrable mystery.

Fantômas! And now the name of Fantômas was associated with the scandal brought about by Frederick-Christian!

M. Annion slept badly, haunted by a nightmare in which he was constantly pursuing an extraordinary Fantômas, whom he would seize and bind and who would then suddenly vanish into thin air. At eight o'clock in the morning he appeared at his office. There a surprise awaited him. Upon his desk lay a telegram. Rapidly tearing it open, he glanced at the text.

"Ah!... Good God! Can it be true! Fantômas dead! Fantômas dead in prison! I must be dreaming!"

While he was rereading the astonishing news, the door of his office opened and Juve walked in.

"Juve!"

"Myself, Chief."

"Well!"

"Well," replied Juve, calmly, "I've had a pretty good trip."

Brandishing the telegram, M. Annion cried:

"Fantômas is dead!"

"Yes ... Fantômas is dead."

"What have you found out?"

"Oh, a thing or two ... rather interesting."

"And the diamond?"

"Stolen, Chief, disappeared."

"Stolen by Fantômas?"

"Yes, by Fantômas."

"It was you who arrested him?"

"Hum! — yes and no....I was the cause of his arrest."

"And the murder of Susy d'Orsel?"

"It was committed by Fantômas."

"You are sure of that?"

"Certain, Chief."

M. Annion rose and paced up and down in great excitement.

"Now then, let's get the facts in the case, tell me in detail what occurred at Hesse-Weimar."

Juve had had the foresight to prepare a report which would tell enough to prove that the murderer of Susy d'Orsel was really Fantômas, and thus clear the name of the King. He gave no hint, however, that Fandor was still, as Juve thought, impersonating Frederick-Christian, and made no mention of his own adventures. He concluded by saying:

"In a word, we have now only to establish the guilt of Fantômas and publish the story of his crime, to absolve the King in the eyes of all ... and that will mean the end of your troubles."

"That is true!" replied the director joyfully, "and I may add it is entirely due to you, my dear Juve. Why, the other day, I was actually on the point of arresting Frederick-Christian, which would have been an unpardonable blunder."

"Really?"

"Yes. For since your departure, the identity of the King has been established beyond dispute. Yesterday I learned that the director of the bank had had an interview with him, and he also received a visit from an intimate friend, an attaché of the Embassy."

Juve heard these words with growing uneasiness. The King was Fandor. How had Fandor managed the affair?

M. Annion continued:

"And what do you think happened yesterday afternoon? I received a visit from a little idiot called Marie Pascal, who still insisted on the imposture. She asserted that the King was no longer the same."

Juve felt his head swimming.

Marie Pascal had paid one visit to Fandor, and now declared he was no longer the same! So Fandor was not at the Royal Palace. Who had taken his place?

The real King?

Was Fandor himself a victim?

"By the way," pursued M. Annion, oblivious of Juve's trouble, "you didn't happen to learn any details concerning the King's toilette at Glotzbourg?"

"No, why?"

"Oh, nothing of importance. I should like to have known whether it was a fact that Frederick-Christian wore an 18-inch collar. It would merely have been another proof."

The words literally stupefied the detective. If the man at the Royal Palace wore 18-inch collars, he was certainly not Fandor, whose neck was very slender. The journalist wore size 14-1/2.

One hour later — it was then half-past ten in the morning — Juve arrived at the Royal Palace. He did not attempt to send up his card to the King, but contented himself with gathering what information he could from among his colleagues who were stationed about the hotel.

"The deuce!" he cried, twenty minutes later. "It's true that Frederick-Christian is really here. What has become of Fandor? Well, I shall probably be able to get news of him at his own apartment. What I have to do now is to recover the diamond and catch Fantômas ... if that is possible."

CHAPTER XXV
"I WANT TO LIVE!"

During two days which passed like two centuries, Fandor had been held prisoner in his dungeon where death awaited him.

"I am condemned to death," he exclaimed, "very good, then I will wait for death."

But Fandor was of those who do not give up until the struggle is over. Besides, he had his faithful revolver. He could end his life at any moment and shorten the torture. He had found sufficient ham to last for two meals, and when that had been eaten and the last drop of water drunk he began to suffer the tortures of hunger and thirst. And now, like a caged beast, he paced up and down his prison. His mind went back to stories he had read, stories of entombed miners, of explorers hemmed in by ice, of hunters caught in traps, but in all these cases deliverance in one form or another had come at last — the adventures ended happily.

"I want to live," he cried aloud, "I want to live!"

Suddenly a great calm descended upon him. His coolness and clear judgment returned.

"To struggle! Yes — but how?"

At this moment the roar of the Nord-Sud shook his prison walls. An idea took root in his mind.

Might it not be possible to burrow his way through the soil directly to the tunnel! Examining the ground, he decided that it would be simpler to tunnel his way like a mole, skirting the concrete base of the statue and reaching the pavement beyond. It would not be hard work to dislodge one of the paving stones and reach the open air. No sooner was the plan conceived than he broke several of the bottles until he obtained a piece of the thick glass sufficiently jagged to form a trowel.

With this rough implement he then set to work, scooping up the earth and piling it on one side of his cell. Patiently and ceaselessly he continued, hour after hour, until suddenly the hiss of escaping gas could be faintly heard.

"I'm done for this time," he cried in despair. "I shall be asphyxiated!" But a gleam of hope quickly set him to work again.

"Gas is lighter than air. It may percolate through the chinks of the masonry. In any case I'd rather die that way than be starved to death."

It was a race between the escaping gas and the tunnel.

Very soon Fandor began to feel a dizziness in his head, and the air became more difficult to breathe; suddenly, he had the sensation of being enveloped in an extraordinary blue flame, and then a loud report deafened him.

Fandor's prison, saturated with gas, had suddenly blown up!

The ground gave way beneath him: he was lying in the ruins.

Destiny had made a plaything of his efforts.

CHAPTER XXVI
THE ACCUSING WAISTCOAT

"As a matter of fact, Monsieur Juve, did not the celebrated Vidocq before he was a detective begin life as a murderer?"

Wulf, book in hand and comfortably installed in a large armchair, addressed the question to Juve, who answered in brief monosyllables, without turning his head:

"That's true, Monsieur Wulf."

"And don't you think that every detective at one time or another has a tendency toward crime, either as a thief or as an assassin?"

"That I cannot say."

What a day Juve had passed! Events had succeeded each other with such startling rapidity that the detective, in spite of his robust physique, began at length to feel the strain. As a matter of fact he had really had no rest since his tragic awakening in the mortuary chapel at Glotzbourg. He had passed the following night in the train without closing an eye. Upon his arrival he had been busy without interruption until he found himself, at ten o'clock at night, in his little apartment in the Rue Bonaparte with the grotesque Wulf as companion. While the latter was tranquilly reading the adventures of Vidocq, Juve was absorbed in a strange task which occupied his entire attention.

He was minutely examining a queer-looking garment, a waistcoat of very unusual cut. He turned to Wulf:

"Monsieur Wulf, you recognize this garment, don't you? There is no doubt that it came from Jacob and Company, the Glotzbourg tailors?"

Wulf nodded.

"No doubt whatever. I've had too much experience in such matters to be mistaken....Besides, the initials J. G. are on the buttons."

"Yes, yes — Jacob of Glotzbourg."

Juve now examined the lining with a magnifying glass, muttering the while:

"Ah, just as I expected!"

The pocket of the waistcoat had been distended by some large object which had been forcibly introduced into it. The detective quickly took some modeling clay and made it into certain dimensions carefully measured, then with a stick he marked the surface of the ball into facets, referring now and again to a book open before him. "Let's see," he exclaimed, "the Hesse-Weimar diamond is two-thirds of a hen's egg in size, and weighs 295 carats, that is to say, larger than the Koh-i-noor, the famous Indian diamond, one of the crown jewels of England."

He now introduced his model into the pocket and found that it fitted the hole exactly.

"There! What do you say to that!" he cried.

"Why, you're very clever, Monsieur Juve," replied Wulf, "but I don't see how that helps. Even if you prove that the King's diamond was kept for a certain time in the pocket of that waistcoat, still you don't know to whom the waistcoat belongs, and that's the most important point."

Juve, still engrossed in his examination, vouchsafed no reply, and Wulf with folded arms stood contemplating him. Various problems were engaging Juve's thoughts, whose day had been exceedingly busy.

After being satisfied that Frederick-Christian was really back again at the Royal Palace, the question arose as to what had become of him after his disappearance. A hurried visit to Fandor's lodgings disclosed the fact that the journalist, after a brief absence, had returned home for an hour and had then disappeared again.

"Upon my word," he thought, "he might at least have sent me some word. He must know how anxious I would be about him."

From Fandor's house Juve had gone direct to Susy d'Orsel's apartment. It was a theory of his that a good detective could never visit too often the scene of a crime. Mechanically he went through the various rooms until he reached the kitchen.

"I have a feeling that something happened here," he muttered, "but what?"

A close examination of the floor showed distinct traces of feet in some fine coal dust. These traces proved to be those of a woman's shoes, small, elegant and well made. They could not possibly belong to Mother Citron nor to Susy d'Orsel, who, he recalled, had worn satin mules on the night of the murder. The person who immediately presented herself to Juve's mind was Marie Pascal.

"The deuce!" he cried, "this becomes complicated. This coal dust and these imprints were not here a few days ago, therefore some one has been here since and has evidently been at pains to lay a false trail!"

With the intention of examining the servants' staircase again, he let himself out with a pass-key and began the descent. But so absorbed was he in his thoughts that unconsciously he went down one flight too many and found himself in the cellar of the building. Juve, following his custom of never neglecting to search even the most unsuspicious places, lit his electric light and examined the room he had entered.

On either side of the cellar were ranged a number of doors, all securely padlocked. These were evidently the private cellars of the tenants. As he threw his light on the floor, he could not repress a movement of surprise. Dropping on all fours, he began a close examination of the ground.

"Now I begin to see daylight. For some time I have had the conviction that Frederick-Christian, upon leaving Fandor made his escape by the servants' staircase, and thus left the house. But I could not understand why he had not returned to his hotel. My conclusion was wrong. Frederick-Christian, like myself, came down a flight too many and found himself, as I have, in this cellar. Evidently a scoundrel was waiting for him here. The trampled ground, the shreds of silk torn from a high hat, all indicate clearly the struggle which took place. But the King, being drunk, was easily overpowered and bound. That is the reason he did not reach his hotel."

One difficulty still troubled the detective. It had been shown that on the night of December 31st, the third person, otherwise the King, whom Fandor declared to be in the apartment, had been unable to escape by the back stairs, since the door was locked and bolted. Then it came into Juve's mind that the maid Justine in giving testimony had become embarrassed and finally had admitted that the key having been lost, she had neglected to lock the door. This cleared up the dubious point and established in Juve's mind the complete explanation of what happened.

Fantômas, after killing Susy d'Orsel, had lurked on the stairs until the King left the apartment. Then, locking the door, he had hurried after his victim and caught him at the moment he reached the cellar.

The detective's next move was to break into the apartment of the Marquis de Sérac. By the aid of a ladder which he found in a corner, he climbed up and broke a windowpane and thus made his entrance. At first nothing in the apartment seemed worthy of suspicion. The rooms were elegant but commonplace. The bureaus and wardrobes were locked, and gave out a hollow sound when rapped upon. As he did not have his burglar's equipment with him, Juve decided to come back later and investigate. He was on the point of leaving when his foot caught in a garment, which he found to be a waistcoat. He gave vent to an exclamation of surprise as he picked it up and folding it into a bundle hid it under his overcoat. The Marquis de Sérac had been under his suspicion for some time; now that suspicion was in a fair way to become a certainty. Were the Marquis and Fantômas one and the same?

Juve was inclined to answer in the affirmative....

The next step was to invite Wulf to dine with him, to show him the waistcoat and prove beyond doubt that it had been made by a tailor of Glotzbourg.

Juve's opinion had now become a solid conviction. Fantômas had worn the garment, and had carried the diamond in the pocket of the waistcoat he found in the Marquis de Sérac's apartment. Hence the Marquis de Sérac was Fantômas.

CHAPTER XXVII
THE EXPLOSION OF THE NORD-SUD

The Empire clock on Juve's desk struck half-past eleven. The detective, having gone over in his mind the course of events just narrated, rose abruptly and tapped Wulf on the shoulder.

"Monsieur Wulf, if you are to remain here you are very welcome to do so; as for me, I'm going out."

Wulf, wakened out of a doze, sat up and stared at Juve, an expression of dawning suspicion in his eyes.

"Where are you going?" he inquired.

Juve, absorbed in his thoughts, did not remark the strange behavior of his colleague. He had settled on a plan of action, which was simply to arrest the Marquis de Sérac.

"Oh, I'm just going ... for a walk."

"All right, get your hat."

A few moments later the two men hailed a taxi and drove to 247 Rue de Monceau.

During the trip Juve pumped Wulf about his relations with Fandor, and it appeared that the latter had pursued the policy of making Wulf drunk upon every occasion. Doubtless, the detective reasoned, it was thus that Fandor was enabled to escape for an hour, during which time the substitution had been effected. Wulf explained how he had found the King near the fountains in the Place de la Concorde, and Juve realized that in some way or other the King and the fountains were mysteriously connected.

In his turn, Wulf plied Juve with questions as to what he had done during his stay at Glotzbourg.

What sort of welcome had he received from M. Heberlauf?

How had the arrest of Fantômas been effected?

How had the monster died?

The detective, naturally, had no intention of enlightening Wulf as to the truth.

He therefore answered in monosyllables, annoyed by the turn the conversation had taken. In fact, as the questions became more pressing, it flashed through Juve's mind that the stupid officer was actually beginning to suspect him of being Fantômas. As the taxi neared its destination Juve suddenly put his head out of the window and cried with an oath to the chauffeur:

"Follow that automobile which is just starting and don't lose sight of it!"

Wulf turned inquiringly:

"It's the Marquis de Sérac."

"Well, what of it?"

"Why, is he the man we are after?" Then turning again to the chauffeur:

"Have you plenty of gasoline?"

"Enough to run a hundred miles, Monsieur."

The chase began at the Boulevard de Courcelles, continued through the Place de l'Etoile and the Avenue de la Grande Armée. The two taxis, of the same horsepower, kept an equal pace, but the Marquis de Sérac's chauffeur seemed the smarter man. At any rate, he was the more daring. He dodged in and out of the traffic and began to gain on his pursuers.

"He's taking us to the Bois," growled Juve, as they made a turn to the left after passing the fortifications, before the Barrière de Neuilly. The pace increased in the back streets and then, suddenly, the taxi of the Marquis de Sérac disappeared!

It had turned sharply down a narrow street.

At the risk of his neck, the detective sprang out of his taxi and rushed round the corner, just in time to hear a door bang to.

Wulf now joined him.

"We have wasted our time, my dear Juve. The taxi we have been following was empty. It made a circuit and passed me just now."

"Just what I expected!" cried Juve, "our man got out of it ... he is still here."

Juve took out his revolver, and then an exclamation of surprise escaped his lips. Fifty yards away, a figure appeared, vague and dressed in white.

"What the devil does that mean? I've been following the Marquis de Sérac, of that I'm sure, and now I find this other one." Then turning to Wulf, he gripped him by the arm. "You see that individual, well, he is the Primitive Man Ouaouaoua."

Taking the utmost precaution, Juve and Wulf followed the enigmatic Ouaouaoua for over an hour. The singular meeting had given the detective food for thought. This man had figured prominently at the ceremony of the Singing Fountains; again, he had been foremost in the demonstration of the mob against the King outside the Royal Palace. It was now that a suspicion came to Juve's mind, that this venerable beard and white woollen robe concealed the person of the Marquis de Sérac.

"Whatever happens," he muttered, "I must get to the bottom of this. While it would be quite easy to bring him down with a shot from my revolver, yet, once dead, I could get no information from him."

They arrived at the corner of the Boulevard Malesherbes and the Avenue de Villiers, and Juve's excitement grew, for he knew that not far away was the America Hotel, where Lady Beltham had put up under the name of the Grand Duchess Alexandra. Ah! If it were possible to connect the Primitive Man with her! In that case he would not hesitate to arrest them both, although he suspected that Fantômas's mistress would be more ready to give him up than to shield him.

But Ouaouaoua brusquely made a right-about face and headed toward the Boulevard des Batignolles.

"Are we going to keep this up much longer?" inquired Wulf, who by this time was breathless and weary.

"You can go if you like," growled Juve without turning his head. In his intense absorption, Juve failed to notice the menacing and ironical look the officer directed at him.

Ouaouaoua now turned down the Rue Notre-Dame-de-Lorette hastening his speed. The two men had some difficulty in keeping up with him. Suddenly he disappeared at the corner of the Rue Saint Lazare and the Rue Lamartine. Juve sprang forward just in time to see the white draped figure vanish down the stairs leading to the underground Station of the Nord-Sud.

The Station was lighted and the ticket windows open. The morning's traffic had begun.

"Have you just seen a queerly dressed man?" he asked one of the porters.

"He has just bought his ticket, Monsieur."

Juve flung down a coin, seized two coupons and without waiting for the change hurried onto the platform. The first morning train was waiting, due to start in five minutes. A quick search through the carriages disclosed the object of Juve's search. He was standing in the first carriage by the door of the driver's compartment. While Juve eyed him eagerly, the Primitive Man in turn was watching the detective.

The conductors and employés were standing gossiping by the ticket office, and the station was almost deserted at this early morning hour.

Juve remained on the platform with Wulf. As a preliminary to making his arrest, he took out his revolver, and held it in the palm of his hand. Suddenly he gave a yell and sprang forward. Ouaouaoua, taking advantage of the engine driver's absence, had entered his compartment and pulled the levers.

In a moment the train was under way. As Juve made a jump on board, Wulf tried to restrain him, and in the scuffle knocked the revolver out of the detective's hand. To the consternation of the train's crew left behind in the station, the train was now gathering speed. Their shouts in turn alarmed the few passengers, who regarded the precipitate entrance of Juve in amazement. Finally a cry from the powerful lungs of Wulf was heard above all the other noises. A name shouted in terror:

"Fantômas!"

A rush was instantly made to seize the fool or the madman who had started the train, but a revolver shot quickly drove back the passengers and Juve, furious with the imbecile Wulf for having disarmed him, was obliged to take cover with the others.

The train passed through the Station de la Trinité, shot through Saint Lazare without heed to signal and tore along at headlong speed. And then, in a moment, the train was plunged into total darkness and a cry of rage escaped from the Primitive Man. The detective understood in a flash.

The Nord-Sud had had the happy idea of cutting off the power, and Juve noticed that this occurred just as the train had passed the Station de la Concorde and entered the tube beyond. Ah! this time the Primitive Man was in a tight corner. His revolver would be less dangerous in the darkness.

Juve rose carefully, prepared to advance, when a spark was seen, succeeded by a terrific explosion. A shower of matter fell upon the train, shattering the windows and throwing the passengers pell-mell upon each other.

Then ... silence....

The red lights of torches gradually lighted up the tunnel in which the tragic accident, still unaccounted for, had occurred. Juve, unconscious for ten minutes, came to his senses and realized with a sense of relief that he was unhurt, and that the men directing the rescue were the Paris firemen. Many persons had been wounded, but by an apparent miracle not one had been killed.

The Primitive Man had disappeared.

Juve, in quest of clues which might lead to the discovery of the explosion, climbed upon the train to where an immense hole in the roof of the tube had showered down bits of asphalt and broken earth. He noticed quickly that communication had been opened with the Place de la Concorde. By dint of hoisting and scrambling he succeeded at length in gaining the surface of the ground.

Vague groanings came from the mass of stones piled not far away. As he approached these noises, they became more distinct. Finally, he discovered the body of a man wedged between two large blocks and covered with a piece of gas-pipe.

The body was begrimed with soot and mud. Juve, after hauling his burden to the open air, where he was greeted with cheers by the crowd, dipped his handkerchief in the water from the fountain and wiped the man's face. Suddenly, he dropped to his knees with a cry:

"Fandor! It's Fandor!"

CHAPTER XXVIII
INNOCENT OR GUILTY?

Juve and Doctor Gast were talking in low tones in the dining-room adjoining the bedroom. Their patient, Fandor, had just wakened and had cried out:

"I'm dying of hunger!"

It was about nine o'clock in the morning. After rescuing his friend Fandor from his perilous situation, he had taken the unfortunate journalist to his own home in Rue Richer and called in a physician of the quarter, Doctor Gast. An examination of the patient showed that he had received no serious injury, merely some abrasions and one or two burns.

As Juve and the Doctor answered his call for food, Fandor sat up and without surprise or question repeated his cry:

"I'm dying of hunger. Hurry up and give me something to eat."

The Doctor took his pulse, then suggested:

"Something light won't hurt him, say, a slice of ham."

A formidable oath was the reply:

"No, thanks!... anything you like, but not ham."

"All right ... a chicken wing instead."

This seemed to satisfy Fandor, who added:

"While I'm awful hungry, don't forget that I'm just as thirsty!"

"Well, Doctor?"

"Well, Monsieur, I find everything going well. Our patient has had a good meal and is now sleeping peacefully. By to-morrow, M. Fandor will be all right again. It was, however, about time he got food, for in my judgment he pretty nearly died of hunger."

"That's what I can't understand."

"When you went back just now to the scene of the accident, didn't you learn any of the details?"

Juve answered evasively:

"Nothing to speak of, Doctor, merely that the wounds of the passengers are not serious. As to the cause of the explosion, I have a notion that it may have been due to an escape of gas. I noticed a strong odor of it about. Probably a spark set it off."

The doctor now took his leave, and no sooner was he well out of the door when a joyful whistle came from the sick man's room. Juve could not restrain an exclamation of surprise as he looked into the bedroom. Fandor was already partly dressed and in the act of lacing up his boots.

"You are crazy to get up in your condition!"

"Hang my condition, I feel as strong as a horse and as hungry as a bear."

Juve laughed.

"Oh, if that's the way you feel there's nothing more to be said."

After a second breakfast, Fandor turned to his friend:

"Now, then, Juve, let's hear where you've been!"

For two hours each in turn narrated their adventures of the past days, and by combining their experiences, they arrived at a clear view of the situation. One question was answered beyond doubt. The hand of Fantômas was everywhere apparent. His carefully laid plan to get possession of the King's diamond unquestionably involved the arrest of the King by the French authorities for the murder of his mistress.

It was now their difficult task, first to recover the jewel and then capture the bandit. Two points still remained to be cleared up. What rôle had Marie Pascal played in the affair? Was she innocent or an accomplice? And had Lady Beltham intended to save Juve or had she intended to save Fantômas?

It was finally arranged that Juve should go to the America Hotel and call on the pseudo Grand Duchess Alexandra, and that Fandor should see Marie Pascal. They were about to put this project into execution when a loud knocking at the door startled them.

Fandor sprang forward, but the detective quickly thrust him into the bedroom, and opened the door himself.

"You here, Wulf!"

"As you see."

The absurd officer marched into the apartment with an air of great satisfaction.

"Well, Monsieur Juve, and what do you think of my detective instinct?"

"I don't understand."

"Ah, you thought you'd got rid of me at the Sud-Nord Station, didn't you, but I fooled you. I arrived at the scene of the explosion at the precise moment you were giving an address to the chauffeur and carrying away a body."

"A body ... in pretty good health!"

"Furthermore, I came across some one you were looking for, I think."

"Fantômas?"

"No, not Fantômas, but the Primitive Man, generally called Ouaouaoua."

"And you let him go?"

"Oh, I let him go all right, but not before he gave me his address."

Juve smiled grimly.

"A nice mess you've made of it!"

Wulf continued with an air of great importance:

"I can tell you something else, the King returns to Glotzbourg to-night, but before he goes we shall have the guilty person arrested."

A slight noise made Wulf turn his head and then give a loud cry.

Fandor had entered the room.

"Good God! Who is that?... the King?... No, it's not the King ... help! help!"

Wulf cast frightened glances to right and left and then made a dive for the door, slamming it behind him as he rushed out:

"I knew he was a fool," exclaimed Juve, "but I didn't know he was crazy besides. And to think he had Fantômas in his hands and let him go!"

The two men now reverted to their interrupted project and decided to pay their respective visits to Marie Pascal and Lady Beltham.

"Mam'zelle Marie! Mam'zelle Marie! Come in and rest a bit!"

The pretty lace-maker was passing the office of the concierge, the so-called Mother Citron. The young girl accepted the invitation and sat down, heaving a deep sigh. It was only ten in the morning but her red eyes and her face showed signs of having passed a bad night.

"You mustn't work so hard!" exclaimed the concierge.

"Oh, it isn't my work; that rests me, it helps me to forget....I have so many troubles."

"Tell me all about them."

By degrees and through her tears, Marie confided all that had happened to her since the night of the murder. The avowal of love she had made to the King and the unforgettable hour she had passed in his company; then the police inquiries, suspicions, and the fact that they were continually following her.

"Ah, if only I had some one to turn to. I've thought of going to see this detective the King spoke of, M. Juve."

As Marie Pascal pronounced that name, an expression of sinister joy came into the eyes of Mother Citron:

"That's a good idea," she exclaimed.

Marie hesitated:

"I would never dare go to see him alone."

"Marie Pascal, you know how fond of you I am, and as sure as I'm called Mother Citron, I'll prove what I say. In a couple of minutes I'll put on my hat with the flowers and leave my workwoman in charge here. Then I'll take you myself to this M. Juve... if you're afraid of him, I'm not!"

CHAPTER XXIX
COMPROMISING DISCOVERIES

Fandor, smoking a good cigar, walked to the Rue Monceau, taking deep breaths of the fresh air, looking up with delight at the blue sky. After his imprisonment and slow torture he experienced an extraordinary joy in living and in his freedom.

When he reached the house he found the concièrge's office empty. He called out several times.

"I'm the concièrge, what is it you want?" a voice answered behind him.

Fandor turned sharply:

"Ah, there you are, Madame, I didn't see you."

It would have surprised the journalist had he known that the extraordinary Mme. Citron a moment before had been comfortably installed in the Marquis de Sérac's apartment, and that hearing herself called, she had slid down her communicating post to answer the summons. Still further was he from imagining that the Marquis de Sérac and Mme. Citron were one and the same person.

"Well, now that I'm here, what is it you want?"

Madame Citron recognized Fandor. But she recognized him as being some one he was not. She had, indeed, only seen him for a few moments immediately after the murder of Susy d'Orsel.

"I want to see Mlle. Marie Pascal. She lives here, doesn't she?"

"Yes, Monsieur, but ..."

"Is she at home?"

"What is it about?"

Fandor answered casually:

"I have an order to give her."

"Then, if Monsieur will leave it with me..."

"Why? Isn't Mlle. Marie Pascal here?"

"No, Monsieur."

"Will she be long away?"

"I'm afraid she will."

"All right, I'll come back about six o'clock. I must see her personally, I have a number of details to explain."

Mme. Ceiron shook her head.

"I don't think you'll find her."

"Why not?"

"Well, she's in the country."

"Will she be away for several days?"

"I expect so."

Fandor decided to burn his bridges.

"Look here, it's not about an order; I'm sent here by Juve, you know him?"

"The detective?"

"Yes, Madame, the detective."

Madame Ceiron appeared to be very disturbed.

"Oh! I shall get jaundice from all this bother. I can't even sleep in peace. It'll end in them suspecting me, I know it will."

"No, no, Madame, I assure you...."

"After all, I'd rather tell you the exact truth, then you can't complain of me. You see, it's this way: Yesterday the little girl came and said to me, 'Madame Ceiron, I'm so upset and unhappy, and I'm bothered to death with questions, too, and then, this King who isn't a King ...I've a good mind to pack my trunk and go away.' So I said to her, if that's the case, go by all means — she had paid a quarter's advance — and when you are ready just come back — and that's all there is to it, Monsieur."

"You have no idea where she went, Mme. Ceiron?"

"Well, I heard her tell the cab-driver to take her to the Montparnasse Station."

"Do you know if she has any friends or relations in the country?"

"Ah! — that's a good idea, Monsieur, now I come to think of it, she always went on her holidays from the same station, probably to visit some of her family, but where they live I haven't the least idea."

Fandor had an inspiration.

"Maybe she has received letters which will tell us! Have you the key of her room?"

"Yes, I have the key; would you like to go up?"

"Of course! — I must make a search through her belongings."

Jerome Fandor felt strangely agitated in entering the simple room of the young lace-maker. It has been frequently said that the souls of people can be divined from the atmosphere of their homes, and if this is true, the journalist was surely not mistaken when at the Royal Palace he had experienced a rather warm feeling for Marie Pascal.

The room showed no sign of precipitate abandonment, nor any preparation for a long absence. Her work-basket and cushions were all in place, and one would have expected her return at any moment. But alas! Fandor could harbor no illusion regarding her. Her flight was evidently to escape a probable arrest by Juve. A minute inspection of Marie's papers disclosed nothing of importance; but upon opening the last drawer in her desk he found, hidden under envelopes and letter paper, a number of small objects.

"Ah! the devil!" he exclaimed.

The objects were jewels, brooches, rings, earrings and also a large key, evidently of an apartment door. One glance at the jewels was enough. Fandor had seen and admired them upon the person of Susy d'Orsel during the supper which preceded her tragic death.

"My God! there's no doubt now," he muttered, "Marie Pascal is the accomplice of Fantômas."

And then the journalist decided upon a theory to account for her having left the jewels behind. She had probably arranged to have them found among somebody else's things and thus to throw suspicion from herself, just as she had attempted to leave the famous chemise in the Marquis de Sérac's laundry.

"What will Juve say to this? I must see him right away!"

He turned to the concièrge:

"Madame Ceiron, I realize our search here will be without result, so I will leave you now and probably return about ten to-night with my friend Juve."

"Very good, Monsieur. You found nothing, I suppose?"

"Nothing at all," declared Fandor.

While Fandor was going downstairs the pseudo Mme. Ceiron made a grimace.

"He's found nothing, hasn't he? And yet he's turned over everything I left in that drawer! He's not so clever as Juve, although he isn't a fool.... After all, I don't care, I've got them both where I want them."

Jerome Fandor shouted an address to his driver:

"Rue Bonaparte, and if you hurry there's a good tip waiting for you."

CHAPTER XXX
SHADOWED

An unusual cold had continued for nearly a week, and the ice fête organized by the skating club upon the upper lake in the Bois de Boulogne had been announced for this particular day. This fête had been already frequently postponed on account of the weather. It had become a joke among Parisians to receive an invitation for a date which was invariably followed by a period of thaw, turning the lake into ice water and mud.

And now the afternoon of this January day, which began with the explosion in the Sud-Nord tunnel, had been finally decided upon. The clear atmosphere and severe cold promised no further disappointment. The fête was to be given in aid of the poor of the town and the admission fee was put at a high figure for the purpose of drawing a fashionable crowd and keeping out the mob. Vehicles of all kinds drew up and were parked by the shore of the lake, giving the place the appearance of a fashionable reception.

M. Fouquet-Legendre, President of the Committee, stood chatting with the Marquis de Sérac, and both men cast frequent glances in the direction of the town.

"You are sure he will come?" M. Fouquet-Legendre inquired for the twentieth time.

"You may rely upon it, His Majesty himself promised to honor with his presence the reunion organized by your Committee."

M. Fouquet-Legendre moved away to superintend the preparation of a lunch table containing sandwiches, cakes and champagne. The Marquis de Sérac sauntered among the crowd, exchanging bows and handshakes with his numerous friends.

To see this elegant old gentleman, jovial, smiling, without an apparent trouble in the world, it would be hard to imagine that he was the formidable and elusive Fantômas.

The arrival of a superb limousine aroused the curiosity of the crowd. A distinguished-looking man, wearing a striking cloak and a cap of astrakhan, stepped out of it.

It was King Frederick-Christian II. The worthy president immediately suggested a glass of champagne, but the King made it quickly known that he had come to skate, and desired to remain officially incognito.

Frederick-Christian had regained his popularity in the eyes of the Parisians. The suspicion of murdering his mistress which had attached to him had gradually given way to the belief that he was innocent, and the real perpetrator of the crime was now supposed by the public to be Fantômas.

The King proved himself to be an expert skater, and under the respectful gaze of the crowd, described graceful curves and difficult figures upon the ice. At length the attention of the King was drawn to a woman, who, equally clever, seemed to be amusing herself with copying his evolutions. The figure of this woman seemed not unfamiliar to him, and he finally set himself to follow her, increasing his speed, until the two brought up face to face. Involuntarily a name escaped his lips:

"The Grand Duchess Alexandra! You here, Madame!"

He could not forget that this woman, with all her seductive charm, was actually a redoubtable adversary of his dynasty. The pseudo Grand Duchess, however, manœuvred skilfully, affecting such a timid and embarrassed air that by degrees the King's severity melted under her charm. She seemed a little tired and out of breath from the chase, and when she glanced round in search of support, he could scarcely do less as a gallant man than offer her his arm.

Profiting by this chance, the adventuress adroitly whispered her regrets at the unjust scandal and calumny which had coupled her name with that of Prince Gudulfin.

"Sire," she finally murmured, "give me the opportunity of proving my devotion."

The two, separated from the others, slowly skated away together. Suddenly the King stopped short; he realized he had listened with close attention to the confidences of the troubling person he still took for the Grand Duchess.

What had she been saying to him?

A few minutes later Frederick-Christian, deciding it was time to return to his Hotel, skated toward the bank. The Grand Duchess made a deep curtsey and ended her conversation with these words:

"Sire, may I beg your forgiveness for one of your subordinates?"

"It is granted, Madame ... if what you tell me comes true...."

"Your Majesty will permit me to be present at the Gare du Nord when you leave this evening."

A taxi arrived at the lake. Juve sprang out of it.

The detective bit his lip and swore upon seeing a superb limousine in which he saw seated Frederick-Christian and the Marquis de Sérac.

"Too late again!" he muttered. "I miss Lady Beltham at the America Hotel; I miss the King at the skating. At least, let me make sure that the so-called Grand Duchess is still here."

A thorough search on the ice and among the crowd on shore failed to discover the lady, who had doubtless left at the same time as the King. While skating from group to group Juve was brought up by a conversation in low tones between M. Annion and M. Lepine. Hiding behind a tree, he listened attentively.

"Well, you know the last news?"

"Yes," declared M. Annion, "but it seems very extraordinary."

"There is no doubt, however, this Grand Duchess Alexandra should be well posted ... now. She has formally promised the King that his diamond will be found in the possession of our man ... who will be under arrest this evening...."

"You believe that?" questioned M. Lepine, with a skeptical smile.

"Well, I believe in the arrest — that is certain; but whether we shall find the diamond is another matter."

Juve's first impulse was to make himself known to his chief; but on second thoughts he decided to keep silent. He had gathered from the conversation that the arrest of Fantômas was imminent. That, of course, was satisfactory in every respect.

The conversation continued and, as he listened, Juve could not help smiling.

"They are all right! They realize the work I've done and they want me to reap the reward of it."

M. Lepine had, in fact, asked M. Annion:

"You are quite sure Juve will be at the Gare du Nord this evening?"

"Quite sure; I have given him orders to that effect."

Juve decided it was not worth while going home to get the order. Evidently they counted upon him to be at the Station at nine o'clock; ostensibly to assist at the departure of the King, in reality to arrest Fantômas.

The detective moved away, there was not a moment to spare. Whatever happened it was absolutely necessary that he should have an interview with Lady Beltham.

In her small oriental salon, the Grand Duchess Alexandra sat chatting with Wulf, about five o'clock in the evening.

"Really, Monsieur Wulf, you are an extraordinary man, and your intelligence is amazing."

"Madame is too indulgent," replied Wulf, beaming.

"Oh no, I am only fair to you; I know you are a man of value and that is why I have been at pains to re-establish you in the good graces of your sovereign."

Since her return to the America Hotel, Alexandra had been exceedingly busy. To begin with, she had received a visit from her lover, the Marquis de Sérac. A long conversation in low tones had taken place, and the Marquis had left her, nervous and agitated. The adventuress had then put on a smiling face to meet the ridiculous Wulf, and after some mysterious and complicated business with him had been transacted, she had ended by loading the officer with outrageous compliments and saying:

"And now, thanks to you, Monsieur Wulf, the elusive Fantômas is about to be arrested. Be assured the King will give you the very highest proof of his gratitude for this service. Your position at the Court of Hesse-Weimar will be more important than ever."

Night had fallen and the lamps of the Paris streets were lit up.

At the corner of the Boulevard Malesherbes and the Avenue de Villiers, not far from the door of the America Hotel, a man was seated on a bench; he seemed to be merely resting; but in reality he was closely watching each individual who entered and left the Hotel.

This man was Juve.

He began rubbing his hands with a satisfied air.

"Good, good! The evening is beginning well.... There is one important thing for me to do now; shadow Lady Beltham, and not lose sight of her for a single moment, from the time she leaves this Hotel until...."

CHAPTER XXXI
THE DEATH WATCH

In her ears an incessant buzzing. On her throat a weight which stifled her. In her mouth a gag which obstructed her breathing and tore her lips. Over her eyes a heavy bandage. Her arms were bound at the wrists, her body was bruised by heavy thongs, and her ankles bleeding from the pressure of cords.

Marie Pascal was gradually regaining consciousness. She tried to make a movement, but her body could not respond; she wanted to cry out, but her voice died away in her throat. At first she thought it was all a nightmare, then memory returned and she recalled every detail of her strange and sinister adventure.

She saw herself starting with Mme. Ceiron to call on Juve. The concièrge had said:

"Don't worry, my dear, I know the way. Monsieur Juve gave me his address."

At length, after a long walk, Mme. Ceiron made her climb the stairs of a decent looking house. On the way up she remembered feeling faint and that the concièrge had given her salts to smell. Following that came complete unconsciousness, out of which she woke to hear a grim menacing voice exclaim:

"I am Fantômas! I condemn you to death in the interest of my cause!"

She was in the hands of Fantômas!

And then she fainted again, but not until after a flood of light had been let into her mind. In a flash she understood that Fantômas himself must have been the mainspring of the incomprehensible events enveloping the King's visit to Paris. Furthermore, she divined that Mme. Ceiron and Fantômas were the same person. It was she who offered the salts, undoubtedly inducing her unconsciousness. The sound of a steady tic-tac she recognized as coming from a nearby clock. Where was she?

Was she really in Juve's apartment?

With a supreme effort she succeeded in turning her head a little, and in the movement the bandage over her eyes became loosened and fell off. She could see at last!

She found herself bound to a large sofa placed in the middle of a well-furnished room. Before her was placed a monstrous and sinister thing — the menacing barrel of a revolver. Its trigger was bound by a number of strings, each one ending in a nail. These were embedded in lighted wax candles, and from the nails hung a counter-weight.

It was not difficult to guess its purport.

When the candles burned down to the nails, these would become detached, releasing the counter-weights and automatically discharging the revolver aimed straight at her body. Fantômas had no need to return. His infernal cunning had found a means to kill her in his absence.

Marie Pascal calculated that the candles would burn for not more than an hour — an hour and a half at most. The unfortunate girl now began to undergo the agony of waiting for her approaching end. It seemed to her that the candles had been piously lighted for some death watch. When the wax had melted near the first nails, she closed her eyes and a deep sigh of horror escaped from her lips.

"Pity! Pity!"

Suddenly, Jerome Fandor burst into the chamber, anxious to tell his friend Juve about the objects he had found in Marie Pascal's room. Scarcely had he opened the door than he started back in amazement, white as a sheet. Ah! the horrible spectacle of the young girl lying motionless, as though dead, she who in spite of everything, he still found charming. Then realizing the situation, he sprang forward, put out the candles and removed the revolver.

"Saved! You are saved!"

With infinite precautions he untied the ropes and placed Marie's head upon some cushions. She opened her eyes slowly and murmured:

"Where am I? Help! Fantômas!"

Fandor endeavored to reassure her.

"Don't be frightened! Fantômas isn't here; you are saved.... It is I ...Jerome Fandor."

Marie Pascal was seated in an armchair, still very pale, but with courage regained.

"Now, Mademoiselle," exclaimed the journalist, "I beg you to tell me everything....I promise I won't give you up ... time is precious and if your accomplice had tried to get rid of you, it is only natural; you are dangerous for him....Marie Pascal, I implore you to tell me the truth! Tell me, who is Fantômas?"

The young girl listened to these words with growing amazement.

"The accomplice of Fantômas, I!...What are you saying, Monsieur?...Sire!"

Jerome Fandor interrupted.

"Now don't deny it! Look here, I'll tell you the truth. I am not the King."

"You are not...."

"No, but I haven't time to explain that now...you must help me to capture this criminal ... and I give you my word you will not be involved yourself."

"But I am not the accomplice of Fantômas!"

"Then why did you steal those jewels? Why have you the key of Susy d'Orsel's apartment in your possession?"

Marie's face expressed such bewilderment as Fandor asked the question that he could no longer doubt her innocence.

"Then, for the love of heaven, tell me all you know!"

Marie Pascal told a lengthy story. She recounted in detail the rôle she had played in the tragic affair of the Rue Monceau and ended by exclaiming:

"What you don't know is that Mme. Ceiron is in reality Fantômas. Under this disguise he has tried to assassinate me; he assured you that I had gone to the country, so that rescue would have been impossible."

"Ah, Fantômas!" cried Fandor at the end of the recital, "your hour has come! In an hour at most you will begin the expiation of your crimes!"

As the young girl looked doubtfully at him, he added:

"It's time, Marie Pascal! Come with me and see him arrested!"

CHAPTER XXXII
THE ARREST OF FANTÔMAS

"Good evening, Monsieur Caldoni, so you are starting soon?"

"Yes, Monsieur Vicart, it's customary and also my duty, every time a sovereign, a crowned head, takes the train..."

"You stick as close to him as possible until he has reached the frontier. Well, I'm not sorry to see you here," continued Vicart, "for now my job is over."

"And mine just beginning, worse luck."

"Oh! you have only a few hours of it; you travel luxuriously in a special train..."

"One gets tired of that pretty soon. Last week I took the Dowager Queen of Italy to Menton; then jumped to the Spanish frontier to pick up the King of Spain; now it's the King of Hesse-Weimar — to-morrow, who knows?"

The station was decorated gaily in honor of the departing Frederick-Christian. In a private room, a number of the guests, especially invited, were waiting the arrival of the Sovereign.

While M. Vicart, in company with a special agent, made a rapid examination of the station and satisfied himself that all preparations had been thoroughly carried out, M. Caldoni was talking to the station-master.

"The King's special train is to start exactly at 10.17, that is to say, it will follow, at an interval of 10 minutes number 322."

"The 322 is the Cologne express, isn't it?" inquired M. Caldoni.

"Yes, the Cologne express."

In the meantime a vast crowd of the curious who had learned of the departure of the King by the evening papers, filled the waiting-rooms and platforms. Journalists were grouped apart and the invited guests included numerous persons of quality. Among them was Baron Weil, member of the Council of Administration, and delegated to represent it at the ceremony of departure. Lieutenant Colonel Bonnival was also there to represent the State. At the station entrance, M. Havard stood alone, waiting the arrival of the automobile which contained M. Annion, in attendance upon the King.

Making his way noiselessly in and out of the crowd, Juve gradually drew near the front ranks and reached the cordon of special officers whose duty it was to bar the way to the platform of departure. Here Juve ran into Michel, and the two men silently shook hands. Juve was about to show his card, but Michel smiled:

"No need for you to show it, Juve."

The detective now mingled with the guests, and as he reached the reception-room he moved behind a lady who had just arrived. Waiting a favorable opportunity he approached her:

"Pardon me," he began in a dry voice, "one moment, please."

The lady turned sharply:

"Monsieur, who are you? What do you want?"

"I am Juve, of the Secret Service."

"And I am the Grand Duchess Alexandra, relative of the King of Hesse-Weimar."

"No, you are Lady Beltham. I recognize you and it will be no use to deny it."

The adventuress started panting, in her eyes a look of fear.

"Ah," she stammered.

"I've got you, Lady Beltham. The time to pay has come. You are under arrest." Then in a whisper he added, "Where is the diamond?"

There was a silence. Lady Beltham lowered her eyes.

"Better tell me, and avoid the scandal."

"Don't make a scandal, I implore you. I have the diamond with me."

At this moment the King of Hesse-Weimar entered the reception-room accompanied by his friend, the Marquis de Sérac.

Juve could not repress a start. The daring of Fantômas was beyond belief. But his first duty was to recover the diamond. Leaning toward his prisoner, he whispered:

"Hand over the diamond immediately."

The adventuress gave him a strange and mysterious look.

"Monsieur, slip your hand into my sleeve."

Juve obeyed. His fingers instantly closed around the precious jewel which he identified at once by the feel.

"Monsieur, I came here for the express purpose of returning it, please believe me."

At this moment Juve met the eyes of M. Annion, and he realized that the time had come to report to his chief. The detective had three plain clothes men at his elbow; he now turned to them and with a gesture gave the care of Lady Beltham into their keeping. Juve then advanced through the crowded room toward M. Annion and the King. The latter watched him closely and whispered to M. Vicart:

"This time we mustn't hesitate."

In a moment Juve felt his arms seized and pinioned, and then before he could recover from his amazement, he was hustled off into a private room.

"Search him!"

Immediately one of his guards snatched the diamond from his waistcoat pocket. Juve looked up and in the doorway stood the absurd Wulf and by his side the Marquis de Sérac.

"Fantômas," he cried, "Fantômas!... arrest him!" Then in a sudden access of rage:

"Let me go, you idiots! M. Annion, what does this mean? Fantômas stands before you! We've got him, and Lady Beltham, too!"

M. Annion paid no attention to his outburst, but calmly turned to another man who had appeared on the scene.

"Monsieur Heberlauf, do you recognize this man?"

M. Heberlauf, who never could make a decision, hesitated:

"It seems to me ... I don't know ... I think I do. Madame Heberlauf can tell you better than I can."

Madame Heberlauf now stepped forward and in a flood of words, explained to M. Annion that she had no doubt in the matter.

"By a most infernal device, Monsieur, this criminal escaped from his prison, and not content with that, he killed an unfortunate servant, an old porter whom our police discovered the following day in the mortuary chapel of Glotzbourg."

Instinctly Juve was about to protest but M. Annion held up a hand.

"Silence. You will explain at the trial." Then turning to the Marquis de Sérac, he handed the diamond to him.

"We are very glad to be able to return this precious jewel to his Majesty Frederick-Christian II, and I place it in your hands, Marquis, in presence of Monsieur Wulf and Monsieur Heberlauf."

A yell from Juve interrupted him:

"God Almighty! the Marquis de Sérac is Fantômas!... Fantômas, the assassin of Susy d'Orsel!"

M. Havard came forward:

"It's no use, Juve, keep quiet. We know all you would say. But I may tell you that in every place where Fantômas left his trace we have found undeniable evidences of your presence."

When M. Havard pronounced the name Fantômas, a young girl sprang forward. It was Marie Pascal.

"Monsieur," she cried, "Fantômas is arrested! Fantômas, the monster who nearly killed me two hours ago!"

"Nearly killed you? Where?"

"In a house in the Rue Bonaparte."

"M. Juve's house," exclaimed the Marquis de Sérac with an ironical smile.

"And who rescued you?" asked M. Havard.

Marie Pascal turned to identify Fandor but the journalist had disappeared.

Getting wind of what was afoot after reaching the station, he had kept out of sight and listened to the rumors of the crowd. It was with stupefaction that he at length discovered that the authorities had actually decided that Juve and Fantômas were one and the same person!

With his usual quick decision, he promptly made up his mind that he would be more useful to his friend if he remained free. He realized the probability of his own arrest for counterfeiting the King.

M. Vicart offered humble apologies to the pseudo Grand Duchess Alexandra, who accepted them with a haughty inclination of the head, and hastened to join the suite of the King.

The latter warmly thanked the Marquis de Sérac and amid the acclamations of the crowd the train started.

Wulf, swollen with vanity, cried aloud so that everyone might hear:

"It is thanks to me that he is arrested!"

Juve now left with the police officers, shouted at the top of his voice:

"But I am Juve! Juve! Oh! they are all crazy! Crazy!"

In a few moments he was taken to a waiting taxi, while the crowd took a last look at the departing King and his suite. They were saying:

"That's the Grand Duchess and the Marquis de Sérac!"

Juve gave one great cry of distress, while the tears coursed down his cheeks.

"The Grand Duchess! the Marquis de Sérac! No! no! The police have arrested an innocent man and have let Lady Beltham and Fantômas escape!"

THE END

Footnotes

1.   See "A Nest of Spies."

2.   See "Fantômas," Vols. I, II, III, IV.

3.   See "Fantômas," Vols. I, II, III.

www.ingramcontent.com/pod-product-compliance
Lightning Source LLC
Chambersburg PA
CBHW071332130626
46556CB00004B/1857